# MYSTIC DREAMER

by

T. L. SAMSON

**DORRANCE**
PUBLISHING CO
EST. 1920
PITTSBURGH, PENNSYLVANIA 15238

Dorrance Publishing Co
585 Alpha Drive
Pittsburgh, PA 15238
Visit our website at *www.dorrancebookstore.com*

ISBN: 978-1-6442-6924-4
eISBN: 978-1-6442-6321-1

# FOREWORD

*Truth is defined as "a fact or belief that is accepted as true." Reality is defined as "a thing that exists in fact, having previously only existed in one's mind."*

*For some, these lines can be blurred because what we believe to be true is based on our own perspectives from the information we gather from events we experience, even if others don't share the same beliefs. The mind is our most powerful and dangerous tool, it can convince us of anything.*

*The truth is our lives belong to ourselves and it is what each person believes for themselves that really matters. It is their own reality.*

# CHAPTER I

I arrived at Detroit Metro Airport with little time to spare before boarding the Northwest airliner. I was relieved to have a window seat because it allowed me a place to rest my head while my trusty Walkman played relaxing music for me to fall asleep. I always seem to wind up on flights carrying crying children and though I am not technologically advanced with an iPod, the Walkman does the trick.

Once in flight, I found a comfortable position, barely noticing the elderly couple seated next to me who also seemed uninterested in chatting with their fellow passengers. I turned the music on to drown out the child a few rows in front of me. Usually children calm down after take-off, however this little one was not happy and it was obvious to the rest of the people who were now trapped in this flying tin can that resonated her displeasure. After about twenty minutes of endless crying and screaming, with a tension so thick it could be felt hanging in the air, I turned down the music to hear her crying for her blanket as the frustrated mother lashed out. Peeking between the seats in front of me, I saw this lady grab her child and forcefully push her down into the seat.

As if to let the other passengers know that this was no fault of her own, the mother chastised loudly, "I asked if you wanted your blanket before we left and you said no! It's packed and you can't have it until we land!"

I sat there stunned. To think that this child who was less than five years old was supposed to know whether or not she needed her blanket for the flight and the force in which she was pushed into her seat disturbed me tremendously. I kept looking between the row of seats and saw this tiny face peer into view. Crocodile tears fell from big blue eyes with her blonde curly hair held back by a pink nylon scarf. I wondered how anyone could be so harsh to this pitiful little creature. I waved to her and showed her my Walkman. She looked at me for a long moment with curiosity and disappeared from sight.

I thought to myself, *A blanket, a lousy blanket is all she needs and not one person has bothered to help her with this simple dilemma?* I decided I was not going to be one of those people. I got up from my seat and excused myself from my elderly seat-mates as I climbed from my haven in search of a flight attendant. In the back of the plane I located a steward who was loading beverages into a cart and I asked him for a blanket. I was a bit surprised when he asked me why I wanted it. Because of the tone in his voice and his flamboyant mannerisms, I soon concluded he was a Napoleonic homosexual.

"It's for the little girl?" with a hint of deliberate confusion in my voice. Why would you care?

"Oh, is that all she wanted?" his attitude shifting from inconvenience to overworked whining.

"Yes," I was not offering any information or speculation.

Standing on tip-toe, he barely pulled the standard blue blanket from the overhead cabin and began to walk, almost fall, past me. I moved in front of him.

"I will take it to her," gently pulling it from his hand.

I felt she and I had bonded in our private exchange between the seats and felt she would be more accepting of this unfamiliar safety net if I was to provide it to her. With blanket in hand, I approached her row and leaned over the unfortunate isle-seated passenger and her mother.

"This is my special blanket, but it sounds like you need it more than I do so I will let you use it for the rest of the flight. But I will need it back when we land."

She quietly took the blanket from my offering hand as I reassuringly nodded and turned to go back to my seat. She did not make a sound the rest of the trip. I couldn't help but smile to myself as the rest of the passengers began to unwind and visit with each other. I found my comfort zone again, turned on the music, and drifted to sleep.

I was awoken a few hours later by the announcement from the Captain that we were descending and should prepare for landing. Once on the ground, the mother handed the blanket over her seat.

"Please give this back to the nice lady who let us use her blanket." then called out, "Thank you."

Assuming this "thank you" was for me, I called back, "You're welcome".

"You must be a mom too?" was her reply.

I'm not sure why, but I was annoyed by her assumption that I too was a mother and still a bit annoyed with her and the other passengers for not assisting the little girl. Actually, I related more to the child than the parent.

"No, I just know that they have blankets on planes," I sarcastically responded. A deliberate verbal slap in the face for the mother and other passengers, especially those who have flown before, as well as the flight attendants. I left the blanket on the seat along with my anger and departed the plane.

# Chapter II

I awoke early to the sound of a barking dog.

*You gotta be kidding me,* I thought as I pulled the reading light chain on the headboard. Forgetting which side of the house I was in, front or back, I staggered down the stairs and out the patio door with a cigarette in hand. Realizing the continued barking was coming from the front of the house, I went to the front yard where I saw a small dog across the street. He was light brown and had a tail that curled up onto his back. He was medium-sized and definitely not of pure breed, but then who of us is?

"HEY!" I yelled as if to let him know he had interrupted my sleep.

He stopped for a moment, looked at me rather agitated and returned to his to his tyranny of barking. I lit my cigarette and slowly approached him. Upon closer view, he had a pronounced underbite that made it appear as if he did not have any top teeth. His short fur was filthy and disheveled and he had one pronounced white speckled spot below his left eye.

"What's the matter, are you lost?" my tone relaxing more with each drag of the cigarette and changing to concern as he stepped back with his tail between his legs and ears laid back.

He did not have a collar that claimed ownership, but he went to the porch of the small brick ranch that was caddy-cornered to my brother's house. I peeked in the small window that ran the length of the front door to inquire if the dog belonged to these neighbors. There was no light to indicate anyone was awake or home. The gate to the privacy fence was ajar, so I pulled it back.

"Is this where you live?"

No sooner than I got the words out of my mouth when he darted past me into the backyard. I closed the gate behind him and headed back to the house and my bed. Before I was even able to cross the street, he began his incessant barking again and I wondered if perhaps I made a mistake and he did not belong to those people. If not, they would probably not be too happy that this noise-maker was in their backyard. Going back, I opened the gate and out he ran. Pleased to be free, but cautious of my movements.

"Well, I'm not sure where you live but I'm on vacation and I would appreciate it if you would be quiet so I can sleep."

I was hoping that calm reasoning would keep him quiet long enough for me to sleep a few more hours, dissipating the affects of the jet lag and time change. Either I was too tired or he understood me because I was able to steal away a few extra hours of sleep.

# CHAPTER III

I find my brother's house very comforting. The second story is my personal and private abode complete with a full bathroom. The ceiling fan above the queen-size bed provides a cool breeze that tempers the late morning San Antonio heat. The ceramic tile on the main floor was cool on my bare feet as I made my way to the back deck. As I pulled up a metal grated patio chair, I noticed the shaded hummingbird temperature gauge read seventy degrees, which is much different than the weather I left behind in Ohio. The weather at home saw record-breaking snow fall for the month of February and I had more than my fill of those gray days that seemed to last forever.

Filling my lungs with the first drag of a cigarette, I leaned backwards and closing my eyes. I allowed my other senses to absorb my surroundings. The continuous gentle breeze brought the sweet smell of a jasmine bush and soothing melodic music from the various wind chimes that hung from the rafters of the open patio. This, combined with a choir of caged birds singing in the background and the cooing of the wild white-winged doves, was exactly what my psyche was desperately needing.

The subdivision where my brother Hal and his wife Nancy live seems older given all the new construction that has occurred in the past few years. It is appropriately or rather kismet named Feather Ridge. Appropriate because their backyard has three home-made aviaries that house numerous finches, canaries and an African Grey parrot named Smokey. The sweet serenity was broken by a familiar voice.

"Shadow, come."

Knowing Hal was at work, I immediately knew it was Smokey mimicking the call of my brother's sidekick. Shadow is a German Shepherd-Doberman mix, more Doberman being completely black with the exception of tan-colored eyebrows and lower legs. She certainly lives up to her name as she never leaves Hal's side when he is in the backyard. He says this is because "on death row one week and in paradise the next." However, it is obvious that she has a great loyalty and love for him and a special connection that goes beyond rescue from the local pound. Truth be told, I think she picked him. It is Shadow's duty to guard the backyard and the exotic birds that live there. She has apparently differentiated between Smokey and Hal's voice as she does not pay attention to his taunts. Smokey occupies his own aviary which is filled with colored wooden blocks, a rope chain that stretches from one side to the other, a big hanging plastic ball in the center, and several perches near his four food dishes. San Antonio weather is usually conducive for these outdoor pets. However, clear plastic panels and heat lamps running on timers in the winter months ensure their prize stays warm.

"Hello pretty boy. How's Smokey?" my voice in the manner as if speaking to a child.

Sitting on his perch with one leg tucked under his body, he cocks his head and gives the flirtatious whistle.

"Well, thank you. I haven't heard that in a while." With my index finger poking through the wired fencing, "Come here Smokey, I'll pet your head."

Though his wings are not clipped, he made an awkward leap in an attempt to fly and landed on the fencing at eye level, showing his red underlying tail feathers and long claws.

"Good boy Smokey," I crooned.

He says, "pretty boy" again in Hal's voice, followed by a long whistle.

"That's right, you are a pretty boy."

Staring inquisitively, pupils nonreactive, he puffs out his feathers and slowly bends his head towards my finger.

I gently touch his head, "Good boy, Smokey."

This lasted for about three seconds and then he tried to grab my finger with his large curved beak.

Pulling away just in time, "I see you haven't changed much, still temperamental huh?" I decided it was time to move on to view the other winged creatures.

Behind Smokey's home are two other aviaries. The size of a large utility shed, one aviary is home to approximately sixty finches, most of them zebra finches. Unlike the females who have silver and gray feathers and orange beaks, the males are more colorful with bright red beaks, orange cheeks, and stripes on the throat and breasts. The spice finches have a reddish head and throat that tapers into a chocolate color with white underbellies and brown edges on their feathers, falling into a scallop pattern on the breasts and sides. There are also weaver finches which are my favorite. These feathered beauties are pure white with the males sporting long black tail feathers, or mating plumage, that is shed once mating is complete.

Finches are sociable birds that should be kept in pairs or large groups, which is not an issue as they seem to reproduce faster than rabbits. My brother Hal and his wife Nancy take care not to put aggressive species in the aviary so they all live harmoniously in the outdoor home that was built around a crape myrtle tree. There are over a dozen artificial twigs and branch nests carefully placed throughout the aviary for safety and mating. I was looking in the third smaller aviary when I heard a familiar voice behind me.

"Well good morning, how did you sleep?"

I turned, half-expecting to see that it was Smokey speaking again but it was Nancy. I assume either Smokey has difficulty mimicking my soft-spoken, thick Spanish accented sister-in-law or he relates more to my brother Hal. The latter probably being the reason as African Grey's are very intelligent and can mimic just about anyone or anything.

"This is the aviary that Hal built for me. It's perfect for the canaries since there are so few."

It is smaller than the other two aviaries and is made of wood support beams instead of plastic tubing.

"Why the different screening?" I asked.

"Because the wiring on the other cages allows mosquitoes to get in. I lost four canaries because of that so Hal put window screening around this cage to protect the ones that are left."

The four remaining males occupying this home are all bright yellow, but two are crowned and have slightly orange-colored bellies. The crown feathers on the top of the one's head looked like a toupee, brown and black feathers in contrast to his yellow head with a part in the middle. The other seemed to be suffering from male-pattern baldness.

"What happened to his head?" I asked.

"They were in a smaller cage in the house and the other canaries were picking on him," Nancy explained. "It was like they were jealous of his crowned feathers and they plucked them out, making him bald."

"Poor little guy," I chuckled. "I've never seen a balding bird before."

"He seems to be doing better now that we've moved them outside. The home is much larger so they no longer pick on him. I hope his feathers grow back."

Walking back to the deck, careful not to step in a present from Shadow, "I'm sorry I didn't give you and Hal much notice that I was coming for a visit."

"Don't worry girl, you're always welcome here, you know that," patting my shoulder as she walked past and pulled out the wrought-iron chair and took a seat.

I sat next to her and lit another cigarette, conscious of the direction of the rising smoke as she is easily bothered by it.

"I knew we were getting a visitor," her v's sounding like b's.

"How's that?" I asked.

"Because the blackbirds were singing the other day."

I looked at her quizzically.

"My grandmother taught me that when the blackbirds sing, that means company is coming."

"That's right, sometimes I forget you're an Apache because of your thick Spanish accent," I felt a little foolish because the shape and depth of her eyes clearly reveals her heritage as a full-blooded Native American. She is insightful and spiritual, a gentle soul. Qualities I admire and which I had more of.

"I am Apache, but grew up in Monterey, Mexico, raised by my grandparents. They had the choice to succumb to the soldiers and stay on a reservation or keep moving west until they ended up in Mexico. They chose to continue living life as they knew it, living off the land taking only what they needed, practicing their spiritual customs, and using herbs to cure sickness. I can remember my grandmother putting Amaranth leaves on my cheeks, forehead and feet. The very next day I no longer felt sick." Starring longingly into space she finished, "I miss them terribly and often ask my grandmother for guidance. I wish now I would have asked more questions."

"That's awesome, I wish I had that type of spiritual connection or awareness," I responded.

She looked at me for a long moment. "Is that why you are here? Is that what you are searching for?"

"Honestly, I'm not sure," I answered. "Perhaps you could help me?"

She smiled and patted my hand, "I will do whatever I can."

Though I did not know where they came from or the cause of them, I felt tears rolling down my cheeks.

"You relax for now. I will get you a blanket so you can lay in the sun and draw in its energy."

Moments later, she came out with a thick red and black checkered blanket and a broom.

I take the blanket from her, "Thanks, but what is the broom for?"

She laughed, "I'm going to feed and water the birds. Smokey is a biter so I keep the broom with me to keep him away."

Laughing, I spread out the blanket on the thick stiff grass and laid on my back in the middle of it, beckoning the sun to quench my body. Shadow laid next to me as we watched Nancy cautiously enter Smokey's cage, broom in hand.

# CHAPTER IV

I don't know how long I slept but was awakened by the sound of the sliding patio door.

"You should come in out of the sun before you get burned," called Nancy.

A little confused, I slowly leaned up on one elbow, recognizing the aviaries and pink blossoms on the leafless peach tree next to me. Shadow came bounding off the patio to lick my face.

"Okay girl, I love you too. Now help me up," pulling on her thick neck as I slowly got to my feet.

She pranced around, hoping I would take the time to play and panting from the warm weather.

"Maybe later girl, I'm thirsty and need something to drink." I pulled open the patio door and immediately felt the cool air from the air conditioning.

Nancy was standing at the kitchen sink, running water over a colander filled with fresh greenery.

"Whew," as I closed the door with Shadow watching

from the other side, "the sun sure is hot, but that was the best nap I have had in a long time. I need some water. Where do you keep the glasses?"

With hands full of leaves, Nancy nodded towards the cupboard to the right of her, "Second shelf".

I opened the wooden oak cabinet door, surprised to see stacks of white with pink striped Styrofoam cups in the forefront and glass glasses behind those.

"Styrofoam?" trying not to sound like this was an oddity.

"Yes, we have broken so many glasses on this hard ceramic tile floor that Hal finally got fed up. So, now we use Styrofoam cups. If you prefer glass, they are in the back."

"No, this is fine. It probably keeps the drinks cooler anyway."

Changing the setting from crushed to cubes and filling the cup with cold water from the refrigerator, I still thought it odd that they just didn't use plastic cups instead of Styrofoam.

"It looks like you got some good sun while you were out there." Looking at my legs she continued, "I'm glad I wasn't gone long otherwise you would have burned to a crisp in the Texas sun. How do you feel?"

"I feel great, rejuvenated from the sun's rays, but thirsty," as I quickly drained my eight-ounce cup.

She motioned for me to hand her the recycling health store tote bag on the counter, "I ran to the store for some supplies for a physical and spiritual cleansing, that's always a good place to start." Her voice was calming and encouraging as she accepted the tote and began to empty its contents. "For a physical cleansing, an herbal bath. We have basil, oregano, tarragon, bay leaf, organic oats, and sea salt. It's best to use fresh ingredients but if they're not available, dried herbs can be used instead." Opening a drawer, "and cheesecloth and string to hold it all together. The herbs are placed on top of each other on the cheesecloth like this. Seven basil leaves, three bay leaves, three sprigs of oregano, one sprig of tarragon, three pinches of oats, and one pinch of sea salt." Pulling the four corners of the cloth up to form a pouch, "and sealed with the string that is left long enough to attach to the spigot so that the running water is infused with the essence of the mixture while the water fills the tub." She was now holding the pouch up by the end of the string, eyes sparkling. "Once the tub is full, let it float in the water with you."

"Oh, wow." I felt overwhelmed, "I feel so honored." I was beaming that I would be participating in something her native grandmother taught her.

"While you are in the bath, take your time and open your mind. Try not to think of anything or anyone in particular. Gently push aside any concerns that may be clouding your mind. Once you are done, then I have a surprise for you. Another tradition passed on by my grandparents."

I was excited as a little child, "What? What? Tell me."

She chuckled. "No, you have to cleanse the body before the spirit and that is the only clue I will give you."

I could barely contain my excitement as I followed her up the carpeted stairway to my bathroom above. Pulling back the mauve shower curtain adorned with various butter-flies, she took the string of the tied cheesecloth and secured it to the spigot so the water would flow directly over it.

"Now run the water to the temperature you like and enjoy. Press play on the CD player," gesturing to the small black box on the counter, "and stay as long as you like."

As soon as she closed the door behind her, I turned on the faucets and went to the CD player. *Sacred Spirit chants and Dances of the Native American.*

This is so awesome! I pressed play.

# CHAPTER V

The anticipation seemed to make it take longer to fill the tub as I stood naked, staring into the water. Eyes closed, I took a slow deep breath in through my nose, exhaling through my mouth several times to help clear my mind. Give me peace, cleanse me of all negativity and without opening my eyes, I stepped into the warm water. As I lowered myself in, I could feel the water pulling at the invisible negative vibrations that clung to my body like dirt. Slowly I turned the water off. I can hear the slow deep beat of Native American drums and then a chanting chorus and a soft gentle flute. Though I could not understand the language, it sounded like a prayer or pleading. Head bowed, pulling the fragrant scent of the water deep into my lungs, I spread the water-soaked wash cloth slowly over my face, running it down my throat, and around the back of my neck, feeling the water trickle down my chest and back. It feels amazing. Rubbing my eyes and face with the soft cloth, holding it there for minutes, then running it up and down my arms to feed every inch of my spiritually dehydrated skin. I lean back into the tub, allowing the water to embrace me.

The rhythm of the music seemed to increase the more my body felt cleansed and renewed. The timing was impeccable. I thirsted for more, closing my eyes and sliding down the tub, holding my nose to submerge my head. I wanted to be totally engulfed in this elixir. Water filling my ears, all I could hear was the strong beat of the drums and the vibration of the upbeat melody. This must be what it feels like to be in the womb, floating weightless in warm, safe liquid. I did not want this feeling to end and lifted my head several times, just enough for my mouth to draw breath before going under again.

I finally sat up, the music and voices becoming clearer as the water drained from my ears. I leaned back with my eyes closed and imagination open.

What I experienced next, I feel must have been a dream. With the CD playing and me feeling so relaxed and in the moment, I could have dosed off for a bit. Or maybe I have an excellent imagination that was fueled by my subconscious. Either way, I couldn't wait to share with Nancy. I believe I can share anything with her and she won't judge or think I'm crazy. I pulled the water plug and got out to dry off, putting on the robe that hung on the back of the door and, without combing my curly hair, dashed down the stairs to discuss with Nancy what I felt and saw.

She was sitting on the couch reading behind the round coffee table that held a bowl of fresh cut cantaloupe and two glasses of water. Then I began.

She was almost as excited as me, "How was it?"

"Incredible," I took a quick seat in the leather recliner next to the couch. Suddenly feeling hungry, I popped a piece of the sweet melon in my mouth and chased it with a long sip of the icy water.

"The water was refreshing and I could feel its cleansing powers. As you can see, I felt compelled to dunk my head and…" I giggled, "I had to do that several times."

"I do that myself," she smiled and tried to be brief as she was anxious hear of my experience.

"After enjoying the physical feeling, I relaxed and let my mind wander. I must have dozed off because it was like watching a movie in my mind. Like a dream."

Her eyes never left mine as she reached for a piece of fruit. "What did you see?"

"An eagle. It was flying, wings spread, and looking to the side at me. I did not have the sensation that I was flying but somehow, I was at the same level. I could vividly see its dark brown wings bend as it landed on a barren tree that was black with few branches. Its majestic face was clear with a white head, pronounced yellow beak, and curious eyes looking at me. I saw its talons and sharp, yellow, powerful feet. I did not approach it but did notice the surrounding area was desert-like, no grass and just the one tree that that the eagle was perched on."

Eating another piece of melon, I continued. "Just as quickly as it came, this scene was gone and replaced by the image of what I thought was a wolf. Not the typical long, thin wolf as seen in the movies, but rather short, stocky, and gray. It had white fur around the face with dark eyes. There was light snow on its head and the ground, but it was also surrounded by a thick green forest. There was something friendly and playful about it, so I approached. I saw my hands on the scruff of its neck, petting it like I would a dog. Allowing my imagination to interact with this creature, the scene of the eagle returned and I wondered, *Why are you not playful like wolf? He was so serious.* We looked at each other for a long moment then it flew from its perch and began circling closely over my head. I felt it was dancing and so I too began dancing in circles. We danced for a while and it slowly rose higher and higher until it was gone from sight. I thanked the eagle for coming to me and went back to the wolf to offer thanks and I danced, leaping as the wolf watched then playfully joining in, jumping with snow flying up from its paws."

We sat in silence for a few minutes then Nancy began. "I think the beginning represents your trip here to Texas. The atmosphere is definitely Western and the desert is close." Smiling and leaning back into the recliner, she continued. "In my native heritage, eagles are the symbols of insight and perception. I think you will get answers while you are here if that makes sense. You just need to figure out what the question is," she said as if thinking aloud. "You are still tied to Ohio and I think that is what wolf represents. You described him as gray and stocky with snow in its fur. This wolf, a timber wolf, that has the characteristics you described is common around the Great Lakes region. An area that is not far from where you live in Ohio. Wolves live by defined social rules created by a hierarchical structure, much like people. Wolf teaches to trust your own insights and find a new path or journey. To take control of your life."

"Wow, all that? It sure makes sense though. I can't say what the question would be, but I look forward to the journey that gives me the answers."

"That was good instinct to thank the animals that showed themselves to you," she had a smile of glowing pride. "Very few people have the fortune or ability to recognize these guides. I am so pleased that you were able to see so much."

"I can't believe it myself. I didn't know what to expect but it sure wasn't all that!" I was still reeling from the vividness of what I had encountered and Nancy's interpretation. So much so, I barely noticed her come back from the kitchen with what looked like a smoking white cigar.

"This is another one of the many traditions passed on by my grandparents," she blew gently on the glowing tip to encourage a slow, smoldering burn. She motioned me to the middle of the living room. "Come stand next to me: feet shoulder length apart, arms out to the side, eyes closed. Slowly inhale deeply, hold it for a few moments, and release out your mouth. Do that a few times."

I could feel the energy as the scent of sage rose from below my waist and into my nose.

As she circled me, she said, "envision a white light and pull the smoke gingerly towards you, soaking in its' calming, safe, white energy."

# CHAPTER VI

I barely heard the garage door open and, before long, Hal entered through the kitchen.

"It smells like Nancy gave you a thorough cleansing. It's good to see you, sis. How are you?"

I stretched to meet his six-six slender frame for a hug. "It sure is good to see you too. I'm great, in fact, we were just finishing up. How are you?"

"Couldn't be better," he responded with a twinkle in his eyes.

Before anything further was said, there was a distinct, "Yoooooohoooo, Hellooo?" followed by the upbeat six-knock Morse code that hailed at the front door. Before anyone could react, they said, "Don't get up, I was wunderin' if ya'll seen Dawn?" In through the screen door bounded a harried transplanted Southern woman who seemed older than her daily activities would allow. With her attention now on me, "Oh, I'm sorry Nancy, I didn't know you and Hal had company.

I greeted her with an extended hand, "Unexpected company that is. Hi, I'm Hal's sister Bonnie."

She grasped my hand and pulled me close before I could finish my sentence, "Oh, nice to meet ya. I'm Tereasa, I live a few doors down," still shaking my hand, quizzically. "I didn't know Hal had a sister, but then we just moved in a few months ago." She finally released my hand and headed towards the patio door. "I'm lookin' fer my daughter Dawn who sometimes goes off on her own, ya know. Gets into one of these fits. Why she just loves all these birds, they have a way of calmin' her down. She usually ends up here when she's havin' a bad day."

Getting a closer look at her in the natural light of the patio glass, I thought she seemed to be a bit too old to have what I would consider a young child by her nervousness and motherly mannerisms. Turning and blowing out as fast as she blew in, she apologized for the interruption and cradled the door so it would not slam shut.

"See ya'll later. Nice to meet ya Bonnie," she called from the stoop.

"Nice lady," I said to Nancy, encouraging her to fill me in on this neighbor.

"Dawn is her daughter who sometimes ends up crossing over our threshold to enjoy the calming nature the birds exude."

Circling his finger around his ear, Hal chimes in. "She's a little coo–coo, but has a great heart. She wouldn't harm a fly. All the animals in our zoo love her, which is why she's the first one we call to take care of them when we go on vacation."

"I'm not sure what her diagnosis is," Nancy continued, "but I do know she takes daily medications. According to her mother, she has a tendency to stop taking her medications which throws her into really bad manic episodes. She then takes off for weeks at a time and no one know where she is until she calls home."

"That sounds dangerous," I said.

"It definitely can be, which is why Tereasa gets so concerned and upset."

Hal called from the kitchen, tap water running to refill his buddy Shadow's water dish, "She gets by though and it seems someone is watching over her. I like her," he turned off the faucet.

Less than an hour later, Dawn showed up and to my surprise she is a woman in her thirties. Her tiny frame was draped in baggy, dark blue khaki pants and a U.S. Postal knit polo with her name tag hanging down as if looking at the ground. I almost thought she was delivering a package, but the way she moved briskly with eyes twinkling and a smile revealing teeth that seem disproportionately larger than that of her small mouth, I knew she was no guest in this house.

"Hi, I'm Dawn. You must be Bonnie," she patted my shoulder as she quickly passed by me, heading towards Nancy.

With arms out, Nancy embraced her as she walked into a hug.

"Good to see you girl," Nancy said as Dawn began to disengage from the hug. Nancy maintained contact, gently tugging and stroking Dawn's upper arms and shoulders. "You need to stop by more often."

After a brief moment her exuberance returned and she bounced off. "Yeah, Mom said I should stop down and say 'hi'. So, hi." She wound up at the handle of the patio door, beckoning to Shadow as she fumbled with the lock. "Hey Shadow, how ya doin'? I just love her and the birds. Aren't they wonderful?" She asked, looking at me while sliding out the door before it was barely open, which pronounced her tiny, agile figure that much more.

"So that's the whirlwind your neighbor Teresa was looking for earlier?" I asked with a smile.

With genuine fondness, "Yes, a sweet girl. A real heart of gold," Nancy said.

"I don't know why, but I was expecting Dawn to be of a somewhat younger age, like twelve," I said.

"Twelve is a good number, but not her age. It is however, the number years she has worked at the post office. She used to work the counter selling stamps, weighing mail, and special deliveries. Then she went on to taking pictures for the passports, which she thought was a real hoot. Dawn has lived with, or rather her mother has lived with her, for the past two months. I have noticed that her mother can become a little protective of her. Not that that's bad, she just needs someone to watch over her on occasion, but she is very self-sufficient."

I watched her from the patio door as my sister-in-law described this dog-ball throwing, bird-calling nymph as she entered the Finch's home.

"I like her, she has good energy," I said. "Just a bit much of it though," laughing as I took my investigation further by tugging on the handle and going out for a visit.

"Hey Shadow," I coaxed for an easy greeting stepping off the back deck.

You could always expect some kind of attention getting greeting from Shadow Lee. She has a burning obsession with being the first to draw attention from anyone who comes in her territory. The intensity of her greeting is something that is unpredictable and dependent upon her mood or the weather.

"Good girl. Dawn was right, you are wonderful." I rubbed her ears enough to satiate her need for first call and keep her from knocking me down. "Speaking of Dawn, are you keeping an eye on her? Where did she go?" Encouraging Shadow in the direction of the finch's aviary, careful of where I stepped. The beaded door behind the wire swayed in the in the breeze. Standing next to the crepe myrtle branch and just beneath a hanging nest basket, she stood holding a yellow finch loosely in the palms of her hands. Her energy seemed calm but noticeable.

"Aren't they wonderful? I just love birds. Well, I love all animals, but I'm partial to birds."

I did not detect much of a southern drawl like her mother. "So have you lived in Texas long?" I asked.

"I have been here lucky number thirteen years. My mom moved here a few months ago from Georgia. I was born there, but moved around a lot with my father when I was a kid. He's dead now." She kissed the finch gently. "With the way she talks and all, most folks find it hard to believe we are related." She put the finch in the hanging nest above her, "but she needs me and as her daughter, I feel obligated to help her. Hey Shadow," her attention and somber attitude quickly shifted to upbeat before I could respond. "Whatcha got girl?" chasing her through the yard. "Give me that ball," with arms failing. Clearly they played this game of chase before and Shadow loved it just as much as she did. "She'll wear you out," she stopped next to me. Shadow dropped the ball and Dawn scooped it up, quickly handing it to me. "Here, you can play with us. Throw it!"

I wasn't sure if when I threw the ball that Shadow would be the only one retrieving it. She was. I was amazed at the amount of energy Dawn had and now understood why she was so thin.

Hal poked his head out of the patio door and called, "We're having barbecue for dinner Dawn. Would you like to stay?"

"Only if it's your famous ribs," she smiled widely.

"Of course," he confirmed.

She grabbed my arm like a long lost friend, "Hal makes the best ribs."

"Don't forget to let your mom know that you'll be here," he reminded her.

"See," almost in a whisper, "they know how much Mom relies on me. Sometimes I just need to get away and I guess I do forget to call her. Like one time, I jumped in my friend Emily's pickup and before we knew it, we were in Alabama. We didn't know anyone there. It was a road trip, the two of us like Thelma and Louise. But we didn't kill anyone," snorting as she laughed. "It was a hoot, but I forgot to let Mom know where I was and she was really worried. I still haven't heard the end of that one. It was soon after that when Mom moved in. She needs to be close to me."

"That's good though, she seems to really care about you and it is nice to be needed." I tried to be reassuring as we made our way to the patio.

She finally let go of my arm when we pulled out the wrought-iron chairs to sit down.

"How long are you visiting?" she squirmed in her chair trying to control the need to keep moving.

"I'm not sure, a couple of weeks, I guess."

"Until you get yourself together?"

"What do you mean by that?" I now felt self-conscious.

"Because this is where I come when I don't feel so good," she said as she got up from her seat, chasing after Shadow. I was amazed at the amount of energy she had and now understood why she was so thin. She was always moving.

"Dawn, come here for a minute. Your mom wants to talk to you," Nancy called from the patio door, phone in hand.

"Oh yeah, thanks Nancy," she got to the patio door in record time and grabbed the phone as she slid inside. She was on the phone until dinner was ready and from what I could see through the door, she did most of the talking with her arms waiving in the air.

"Let's just eat. She will be out when she's done," Hal said as he grabbed at the ribs.

"Sounds good to me. This looks great," I said as I was filling my plate.

"Yes, your brother is a good cook. Don't let him fool you though, he can use a stove just as well as a grill," said Nancy.

"That's right," Hal said, pointing the rib bone in his hand at me. "But barbecue is my specialty."

Dawn finally fluttered her way onto the patio, grabbing at the ribs before she sat down.

"Thanks again for inviting me to dinner, this is the best." Biting at the rib, she had sauce on her face and a smile so wide it showed the meat in her teeth.

"So," Nancy began, "Hal and I were thinking it's time for a vacation and we would like to take Bonnie with us. If you can watch over the pets Dawn, we would really appreciate it."

"An adventure, how delicious," Dawn said and then winked at me. "I just love road trips. I would be honored to look after the kids. Of course I will have to let Mom help me and all. Make her feel important."

"Yes," said Nancy, "I mentioned it to her on the phone before you talked to her."

She smiled. "You think of everything Nancy," she said as she took another bite of rib meat. "Here Shadow, I'm done," tossing her the bone. "You don't mind if I take some home for Mom, do you?" putting more ribs on her paper plate to go.

"Of course not, there's plenty," Hal offered.

"Okay, see you later." She began getting up and then paused, "Oh, when are you leaving?"

"Probably in two days, if that's doable for you," Hal piped in.

"Oh yeah, that's no problem for me. Have a great trip." With a quick hug, she said, "It was really nice to meet you Bonnie. I want to hear all about your adventure when you get back. And don't worry, I will take good care of the birds and Shadow." She stopped to let the dog lick the barbecue sauce from her fingers before patting her on the head and slipping out the back gate.

"I like her," I said immediately. "A bit high strung but definitely a big heart. So, where are we going?" Enthusiasm filled me.

"Where ever the road takes us," Hal said with a mischievous smile.

"Now you sound like Dawn," I said laughing. "But somehow I think you have more of a plan than that."

"We'll see," He said.

# Chapter VII

That morning, after my cigarette, Hal joined me out on the back porch.

"I planted some herbs for Nancy the other day." He pointed to the tiny plants along the wooden privacy fence nestled in cedar mulch between cactus plants and several potted flowers with solar powered metal flower decorations. "All of them are basil, lemon, cinnamon, and sweet red. The Don Juan rosebush in the back there keeps returning despite several attempts to remove it. So I think we will just keep it, but it needs a trellis to climb. I can make one cheaper than buying it."

Following him into his sixteen foot by sixteen foot woodworking shop in the back of the yard, I asked, "What are the herbs used for?"

"Eating," he replied with a smile as he unlocked the double doors.

I had to laugh at myself, eating them was the last I would have thought Nancy was using them for. Inside, the workshop was impressive.

"Wow, you built this yourself?"

"Yup," he said with pride. "Except the roof, my buddy Reuben helped me with that and the shingles. But I hung the sheet rock ceiling myself and ran the electric from the house. See the air conditioner?" he pointed to the back wall. "It even has a remote control."

"It's actually cool in here," I replied about the temperature as I looked around the shop.

To the right of the door was a generator that provides power for his air tools. Next to that was a floor drill press. To the left of the door was a jig saw with a light attached to the table and a rolling chair, no doubt for tedious work. Next to that there was a table sander for finishing projects. In the middle, a large table saw next to a homemade bench that donned wheels for easy movement. There were cabinets in the back with the remaining walls covered in peg board that held hammers, screw drivers, and wrenches. All of them with several different sizes. I was not surprised to see the large vacuum in the back corner as Hal is very meticulous and clean. He was clearly utilizing every inch of his shop.

"I made this box, what do you think?" He handed me the small wooden box with dove tails and a lid that slid off from the side.

"Nice, pretty fancy for a pencil box," I smiled, admiring his workmanship.

He smiled back at me and took it from my hand, removing a pencil and returning the box to its rightful place on the shelf. Below the shelf was the wood.

"These scraps of wood will be perfect. I just need to cut the side pieces in half on the table saw." He lined the wood up against the blade and adjusting the height and width. "It may get a little loud in here," as he hit the power switch and pushed the wood through the blade towards me. A perfectly even cut. "Now we just need to cut the cross pieces," using the tape measure and marking with his pencil. "We'll use the miter saw for these cuts," now lining up the wood.

"What kind of wood are you using?"

"This is oak," he was always pleased with my questions.

Once cut, he clamped the two long wood pieces to the bench to ensure they did not move. He then pulled out a large plastic case that held his air guns, both nail and staple. He loaded the nail gun and cranked on the generator, attaching the air hose. Again using the tape measure, he marked the spots with his pencil to place the first cross piece. Under his ball cap, I noticed how he would tilt his head to read the tape measure through his transition bifocals, one difference from the boy I would watch as a child some thirty years ago. He also had a mustache now that was almost totally white with age.

I was reminded of when we were children. I was often his uninvited, though not unwelcome, shadow. He would include me in his projects asking me to get him this or that and often "hold it there". He would allow me to follow him and his friends participating in adventures and sporting events. I recall playing football with him and his buddies with the caveat I was not to be tackled. It was two-hand touch for me. But I could handle anything he tossed at me, even his fast ball. It would be accurate to say that growing up, I loved my brother more than anyone. He was always my protector and mentor. I was also reminded of how much time had passed since we were young and how much I have missed spending time with my him. My eyes stung with tears of nostalgia as I stood across from him, trying to avoid his eyes. They were bittersweet thoughts that I wanted to keep to myself.

"I will use this waterproof glue before I nail it together for extra hold," shaking the plastic bottle and smearing the glue. "Then we'll put the cross piece like this," using his small t-square, "and make sure there is an inch over on each side." Grabbing the air powered nail gun, he placed three nails in each side to secure the pieces together. He measured sixteen inches down and marked the spot for the next cross piece and attached it using the same steps. The last rung was closest to me and, as his apprentice, he handed me the tape measure and pencil.

"Sixteen inches down and mark the spots."

I did as instructed, under his watchful eyes.

He added the glue then handed me the nail gun with a smile, "Go ahead, attach the piece."

I took my time and was careful lining up the shots, smiling as I finished. He took the gun from my hand and returned it to its case and putting it back in the cabinet. I noticed that when done using, he returned each item back to its specific place in the shop.

"Will you take the trellis out to the fence? We will wait for the glue to dry and then finish it with Danish oil."

Happy to follow his instructions, I took the trellis outside. He was soon behind me with a cordless drill that he used to make a hole for one of the screws that would attach it to the blocks of wood on the fence.

"You can drill the other three holes," he handed me the drill. "They don't have to be perfect, just as long as they line up with the blocks. The blocks keep the trellis off the fence and allows room for Don Juan to grow around it."

I did as he told me, noticing hardness of the oak wood. When I was done, I handed him back the drill.

"We just attach the screws like so and there, it's done." He stepped back to admire the new rosebush ladder.

"It looks good," I confirmed with a prideful smile.

"Yes, it does," he said as he turned to return the drill to its place in the shed.

I heard the patio door open, it was Nancy was coming to check it out.

"That looks really nice," she said, walking towards me.

"We're going to finish it up with Danish oil when the glue dries," called Hal from the shop.

"That's great," said Nancy. "It looks really nice. You both do good work. Lunch is ready if you two are hungry. You can finish it after you eat, but then I think we need to start packing for our trip. We leave tomorrow."

# CHAPTER VIII

Hal was relying on his portable navigational system he affectionately calls Lola to provide the shortest route to Fort Apache in Arizona. Yucca plants lined the highway in New Mexico with few and farther mountains becoming more visible the closer we got to Arizona. It seems I slept most of the way in the back of Hal's gray Ford F-150 super cab. I recall drifting to sleep to the vocals of James Taylor's "Fire and Rain" and waking up shortly before we stopped to stay in Albuquerque.

Looking at me in the rearview mirror with tired eyes, Hal said, "We're going to get a room, a bite to eat, and stay here for the evening."

"Sounds good to me," I said, realizing I was quite hungry.

"Do you want to eat out somewhere or get something to take back to the room?" asked Nancy.

"We can pick up a few subs and eat in the room," I volunteered.

"I agree," yawned Hal.

Three showers later and with full stomachs, we fell asleep to the sound of the television.

Back on the road early the next day, our first stop was the Petrified Forest National Park, via route 40 which is also route 66. This was an unplanned stop. However, we all agreed we could not pass by the historical brown sign that directed us to this natural wonder. The twenty-eight mile paved road began with a beautiful view of the Painted Desert, which stretched out in front of us for miles. Though the elevation averaged 5,600 feet, the vastness made the appropriately named desert look like pastel waves of light green, pink, tan, and white sand hills. A natural land canvas exquisitely painted by the wind of nature's brush that reminded me of the tides of the ocean.

We passed by the visitor's center and pulled over at Tiponi Point where we got out and stretched our legs. The air was clean and crisp as we soaked in the atmosphere. This point was the first stop at the Painted Desert and afforded us the chance to take either a long or small hike down into the desert. We opted for the latter as we did not have all day to explore the park.

"It's much easier going down than up," huffed Nancy as she drew in a deep breath.

"Amen," was all I could muster, saving lung capacity for the remainder of the climb up the rocky, winding trail.

Returning to the visitor's platform, I sat down on the short concrete rail, followed by Nancy then Hal. Shortly after, a large black bird perched next to me. Close enough to get a good look at its curious back eyes, but not quite within arm's length.

"Is that a crow?" I asked Nancy.

"No, crows are bigger. That's a magpie, a cousin to the crow," sounding surprised by its appearance.

"A magpie? Does it have meaning?" I asked.

"All animals do, right Nancy?" Hal said knowingly with pride in his voice.

"Yes, all animals have symbolic significance. These are curious birds and are considered to be scavengers with the ability to adapt to any surrounding. They are said to be a sign of opportunity for advancement through the proper use of intelligence of what is currently available. It has been said that the magpie is the only bird that would not enter Noah's ark but rather perched on the rooftop. It has also been said that if a magpie perches on the roof of a house, it will never crumble to the ground. It has an association with the spirit world. They are considered spirits in animal form and represent the metaphorical world. There are mixed feelings of luck where the magpie is concerned. Quite interesting," she finished.

"All that from one bird?" I asked in amazement.

"Oh," she laughed, "there's always more. But to learn or understand, a person would have to study their presence and the correlation of the particular time in one's life when they arrive."

"Okay, enough information on the magpie. Let's move on to the next stop," Hal said as he rose from his hard seat.

We all climbed back into the truck to locate the next visitor's area. Continuing on the loop back past route 40, we headed for a different view of the Petrified Forest and landed at Newspaper Rock. With the Painted Desert far in the background, this area called Puerco Pueblo is confined to huge rocks where ancient petroglyphs were left behind from past civilizations that occupied this land some six hundred to eight hundred years ago. The information sign informed visitors that the drawings were etched from the dark varnish coating that covered the lighter rock beneath and included representations of human faces, sheep, antelope, birds, and lizards. Stationary poles with mounted binoculars were available, however most of the petroglyphs were visible to the naked eye. Metal railings allowed visitors to get closer to the drawings, however there were written warnings that oils from human hands damage the petroglyphs and cautioned visitors from touching them.

The longer I looked at the drawings, I couldn't help the feeling of sadness that grew within me. Noticing Nancy's somber expression, I asked, "Are you okay?"

Looking into the distance or perhaps the past she said, "Yes, I feel I owe a respect to this place."

I patted her back sympathetically and left her to her thoughts. I assume we all felt this sadness as we quietly left this once inhabited area to board my brother's truck once again.

The next area was the Tepees, which was a definite change in landscape scenery. This area is clearly visible from the road and consists of large multicolored hills. In contrast to the lighter colors of the Painted Desert, these hills were darkened with colors of gray, blue, white, and reddish-brown. The caps consist of clay with the next darker layers being caused by the high carbon content. The distinct white layers are sandstone with the next reddish-brown layer being iron-stained siltstone. The dark bases are stained with iron oxide which is also known as hematite.

"Where are the petrified trees?" Hal asked impatiently. "This was a forest at one time."

"They must be coming up shortly," I offered, "because I think we are almost through the park. Based on what I have seen so far, I think nature is showing us an order of the park. It's life and death in this area."

Hal's eyes in the rearview mirror encouraging me to continue with my theory.

"It starts with the vibrant color of the Painted Desert, followed by man's life that once lived and thrived here and the dark introduction of the Tepees, which is followed by the ultimate death of nature's life."

He pursed his lips and raised his eyebrows, "I like that."

Sure enough, we began to see a few scattered stone logs along the roadside.

"We must be close," Hal said.

The next sign pointed us to turn left to the Crystal Forest where we found a paved trail that wound through the landscape of the colorful petrified logs. Even in death, these logs were beautiful with the appearance of white, red, orange, pink, and gray crystals encased in the tomb of the bark. Slowly walking the winding path, I could not help but feel a quiet reverence for this once grassland floodplain that has sustained nearly every form of life.

Breaking the silence among us, I said, "This is a sad place. It's like walking through a graveyard."

Nodding their heads in agreement, no one spoke a word.

A graveyard of mother nature's trees of Araucarioxylon, Woodworthia, Scilderias, and others. A bone yard of fossilized trees that once graced this land. Trees that had fallen and were buried by a mix of silt, mud, and volcanic ash. The sediment cutting off the oxygen, slowing the logs' decay. Silica-laden water then seeped through the logs, replacing original wood tissue with silica deposits. Eventually the silica crystallized into quartz and the logs were preserved as petrified wood.

An incredible testament to the life and death of a piece of nature's history. Without words and without stopping at any other visitor points, we left the park.

# Chapter IX

We were approximately thirty miles of winding road from Fort Apache, which sits down in a small canyon surrounded by cliffs. I imagined the Native American scouts on horseback lining the top of the cliffs like in the movies. Not clearly marked by signs and Lola proclaiming, "You have arrived," we finally located the desolate historical site. A wooden sign at the stone drive directed us to the museum and library to purchase tickets. There were two other cars in the small gravel parking area as we pulled up.

"This looks pretty empty," Hal said as he took off his seat belt.

"It feels empty," said Nancy as she opened her door to exit the truck.

The sidewalk led us up to the modern building that posted a huge sign stating that this historical park is owned and operated by the White Mountain Apache Tribe. The Great Seal of the Tribe is proudly in the center of the posting displaying a rainbow over three mountain peaks, a deer, evergreen tree, and stream in the background with feathers and a pot in the foreground.

"Clearly this land does not fall under U.S. law, but rather Indian law," Hal concluded as he held the door for Nancy and I to enter.

There was a plump woman with long black braided hair sitting behind a gray counter that had what appeared to be Plexiglas running halfway up to the ceiling, which I thought was odd. It seemed very cold and institution-like. Her physical characteristics of high cheek bones and almond shaped eyes were and obvious attestation of her identity as Native American. Preoccupied with something on her desk, and with barely a glance, she slid three thickets and a parking pass under the glass after receiving the small fee for entrance.

Though Nancy did not say much, I could feel and shared her disgust as we passed by pictures of American soldiers on the walls. There were very few pictures of the Apaches in their native garb, with the number of pictures increasing with the time that the Apaches came under control of the U.S. Army. Their buckskin clothing was no longer graced with turquoise or feathers, but was replaced with cotton pants and ultimately uniforms when it was converted into an Indian boarding school.

"The brochure says that this army post was constructed to assist the Apache people to remain peacefully on their lands while settlers moved in around them. Nice of our government to take over their land and tell them how to live while the white man came to steal their land! This is such bullshit!" My sarcasm turning to anger.

"I know," was all Nancy could say, slowly shaking her head as we left the museum.

Located in the foothills of the White Mountains, the bulk of this historical park boasts twenty-seven buildings, some made of logs and others of brick. There was the U.S. soldier's quarters which were much nicer than the homes the current Indians inhabit on the reservation. The colonel's home was a large brick building that remained unoccupied. The smaller quarters are made of wood, with some occupied by current natives which was evidenced by laundry hanging out to dry and scattered toys in the front yards. I found myself angry with most of this site, as it was a picture of what the U.S. did to the natives. Hal investigated more than Nancy and I, who did not enter the buildings but rather waited outside.

No longer holding my anger, I complained, "Take their land, build nice quarters for themselves, and leave very little for the natives. If I were them, I would have destroyed these buildings."

"As ugly as their existence, it is a painful part of their heritage and so it remains," Nancy responded calmly.

The White River flowed below the museum and we hiked down a rocky trail to the area where the replicated wooden frames of tee pees stood. We did not stay long as Nancy grabbed Hal's hand and said, "I feel very anxious here, like I was here before and it was not good. I need to leave."

We did not question her obvious apprehension and quickly climbed back up the trail. To the left of the museum was the Sacred Grounds that still held ceremonies. In the eastern part of the grounds was a labyrinth made up of a group of stones that were carefully laid creating a circular path.

Hal read the plaque, "This is considered a powerful spiritual tool whose path can lead to one's own center. They are in succinct geometric form. A sacred design birthed through the human psyche about four thousand years ago. As with life, the labyrinth's ways are complex and winding."

With her first smile since we arrived, Nancy took over. "Yes, the labyrinth mirrors relationships and/or problems, only to find a clue or direction that had not been apparent. You are to enter with your burden and as you circle down the path to the center and back, answers are to come to help solve your problem."

"Let's do this," I excitedly said as I jumped ahead of both Nancy and Hal now standing at the entrance. I started down the circular path, trying to keep an open mind and asking for spiritual insight. I did not see anything or get any answers but then I realized, I don't know what the problem is.

# CHAPTER X

B ack on the road again and Hal broke the silence as we drove. "My buddy Reuben at work said with me being a guitar guy, we should stop in Winslow, Arizona. So we need to back track to Route 66."

Hal's idea of a sidetrack visit seemed to lift our moods. I searched through his CDs and found The Eagles.

"Track 3," I said as I passed the disc into Hal's waiting hand. Knowing exactly what I just handed him, he did not bother to look at the title or wait for the song to begin, when he pressed the button and lowered all of the windows. Looking at me in the rearview mirror beneath the rim of his ball cap, I couldn't help but notice how we share the same brown eyes. Smiling in this moment, serious or inquisitive. It was our eyes that showed the strongest familial relationship. It made me proud. I have always loved my big brother.

"I heard this song was started by Timothy Schmidt of the Eagles but was actually finished by Jackson Browne," he said. Before Nancy or I could respond, Hal turned up the volume and began singing along.

Nancy looked over her shoulder at me between the seats and we giggled and began singing along too. Just like our eyes, neither Hal or I could sing very well but it did not matter. Before the final chorus of "Take It Easy," we pulled up to the famous corner in Winslow, Arizona. *And what a small corner it was*, I thought. There was one stop sign in this tiny town that had two catty-cornered souvenir shops. When Hal turned off the engine and we opened the doors we could hear the famous song being played from speakers just outside the shops.

Exiting from the same side of the truck, which happened to be roadside, Hal looked at me, "I don't think we need to worry about traffic here."

Taking off our jackets, I agreed. "No, I don't think so either. So, this is the historical Route 66?" I closed the half-door and looked down the empty stretch of road.

"This is smaller than I thought it would be. I don't know, I guess I just pictured it as bigger," Nancy said from the other side of Hal's truck.

"I agree," turning to meet her by the tail gate with Hal following alongside.

"Look," Hal said excitedly as he pointed, "a flatbed, red Ford."

"Oh my gosh and look at the building behind it," Nancy said.

"A huge mural," I finished.

"A visual reenactment of the song," said Hal with a tone of amazement. He slowly crossed the two lane road like a wide eyed child at Christmas.

"It's painted to look like a department store front. In the painted windows you can see a table and lamps," now I was pointing.

"Look at the top," Nancy being the third to point, "The illusion of windows to an apartment. See the eagle on the ledge?"

Following her sight, I said, "and there's a couple dancing in the far-right window, wow."

Hal broke out into verse, "There's a girl, my Lord, in a flatbed Ford slowing down to take a look at me."

"So come on baby, don't say maybe, I need to know if your sweet love is gonna save me," Nancy and I finished together.

We all started laughing.

"I see where your mind is! On the woman, huh?" Nancy laughing as she playfully slapped Hal's arm.

"No, look baby. In the mural, the reflection of the girl from the song." Hal sounding teasingly desperate. We all laughed some more.

"Hey, look. A bronze life-sized statue," I noticed over Nancy's shoulder.

Posed with a guitar was the artist who put this town on the map.

"I wonder which artist this is?" said Hal, looking for a plaque or marker other than the "Standing on a Corner" sign posted above its' head.

"Having seen both in concert, I'm sure this is Jackson Browne, not Timothy Schmidt," I said, eyeing the dark features of the statue.

"Let's go in the store for our souvenirs, we can ask there," said Nancy as she headed back across the quiet street.

The bell at the top of the door rang as it was opened, alerting a clerk that visitors have arrived. From the back room a portly elderly woman appeared.

"Hello, can I help you?" she asked, walking towards us, favoring her right leg.

The tiny store was jam packed with memorabilia from The Eagles and Route 66. From t-shirts and bumper stickers to salt and pepper shakers, the owner made the best of the small but long room with items covering almost every inch of wall space.

Hal spoke first, "Hello. We were wondering who the bronze statue is a depiction of?"

"That's from the group The Eagles. I thought everyone has heard of them. Where are you folks from?" She looked at us curiously.

"My wife and I are from San Antonio and my sister is from Ohio," replied Hal.

"We were wondering if the artist was Timothy Schmidt from the Eagles or Jackson Browne, the artist who actually finished the song," I said, sharing Hal's trivia.

With hesitation, the clerk offered her opinion with, "I would imagine it is the person who made the song famous, so I have to go with Timothy Schmidt. We also have Route 66 souvenirs," quickly changing the subject.

"Thank you," said Nancy, keeping us on task. "We're just going to take a quick look around."

We browsed through the store for about twenty minutes and made our purchases. With embroidered t-shirts in tow and feeling mentally refreshed, we quickly got back on the road and back on track.

"I can't wait to see Reuben when I get back to work so I can tell him we stopped in Winslow," said Hal.

"You've been playing guitar for almost a year, haven't you?" Knowing the answer, I was encouraging him to talk about this passion.

"Yup, and getting better," with a prideful gleam in his eye. "Right babe?" as he patted her hand.

"That's right, he's come a long way. I'm very proud," patting his hand back.

I was taken back to last summer. I had no idea he was interested in playing the guitar until we were in our forties. I wonder if he had this interest when I began playing at age twelve. If so, why did he not pursue it? Perhaps he did not want to take the spotlight from the one thing I could claim as my own. It was one of the things I enjoyed as a child. I stopped playing years ago and lost interest. In retrospect, I stopped everything when he and my sister left the house when I was seventeen. I kept my electric Epiphone guitar and dragged it with me from home to home throughout the years, but never played for anyone again, including myself.

Not until twenty-four years later when my brother bought his first guitar and began to learn to play, did I have a renewed interest in playing again. Not to be in the spotlight, but to share a passion. To be able to teach him what I have learned and to be like him in a sense. I am not surprised at how well he has learned so quickly and no doubt he will be teaching me again. The boy and the man were, and are, perfectionists. I wanted to ask him, but some things are better off left unsaid. I also wanted to ask him why there were no family pictures at his house.

Before my mind could catch up with where we were in this adventure, we were pulling into the parking lot of an "Authentic Mexican Restaurant". The stucco building was painted in bright orange and yellow colors, easily spotted from the two lane road. Inside, the tables and chairs were equally as bright with painted parrots and macaws and several layers of a high gloss finish. The food was as authentic as the colorful décor and I found myself exhausted. But not so exhausted I wasn't able to remember my dream.

Native American Indians, faces a blur. There were too many. I saw dancing feet and legs covered in with light skins and moccasin shoes. I was an unseen spectator given the privilege to watch. Dancers seemed like younger males and the elders were in a tent smoking a pipe. I could only focus on one older man. He had long thin gray hair loosely pulled back and was sitting with a wooden pipe. He looked at me and the scene left as if I was only privy to just a glimpse of where they were. The tents were plain light-skinned, like natives' pants. The scene shifted to my winter wolf friend. We immediately began playing. He and I jumping at each other, rolling in the snow. We walked to a field of spring grass and flowers as tall as my thighs. We played very little, mainly walking now. I saw a white wolf with dark brown eyes, a long nose, and a long white flowing tail. She was not playful but mellow, as if she was there to help me rest. I laid with her, my feet at her head and my head resting on her back leg. I was stroking her long white fur. Next I walked towards the east and came upon a beautiful river with green grass and tall trees on both sides. I got in, noticing the water was not cold, but not as warm as my bath water. It was perfect. I began to swim west, which seemed to be the opposite direction the river flowed, but it did not feel like I was moving against the current. I kept looking towards the bank, looking for an animal and then wondered, *Where is hippo?*

Hippo appeared in the water next to me, gray tough skin with pink around his eyes and ears, which were above the water. The rest of him submerged and swimming next to me. We both went under the water and then suddenly I was in front of him, above the water, scratching his chin and ears. I thought getting on his back would be disrespectful but he intuitively encouraged me and I obliged. I pulled myself onto his back, sitting up first then laying on him, hugging him as he continued to swim forward. After some time, I got off his back, said goodbye, and got out of the water to my left.

I was walking in the grass going west when a horse appeared in front of me, dark brown with a black mane and tail. I was not afraid and knew to climb on, pulling myself up by its mane. He began to run as I hugged his back and neck, holding tightly to the mane but not feeling the rough ride one would imagine. It actually felt like we were flying. He ran in the grass for a while before it turned into sand. His footwork incredibly missed rocks and boulders as we rode through the desert-like surroundings. I slid from his back and was somehow then sitting on a rock at the edge of the river. I was now on the right side of the flowing river, head bowed as I poured water over my head. There was an Indian village behind me and I felt I was no longer a spectator, but was seen by them. They did not approach as I cleansed myself in the water, the way I did in the tub. Water was dripping from my head down my face as it cleansed my body and spirit.

# CHAPTER XI

I was excited to share my dream with Nancy, but waited until we were on the road again. It seemed the further we drove into the vast redness of Arizona, the more a feeling of serenity filled Hal's silver F-150. A silent energy that was noticed by all. I could not hold back any longer.

"I had an amazingly vivid dream last night," I began.

"Do tell," said Nancy, as she turned in her seat to face me.

I recounted my dream with as much clarity as I could remember, with Nancy listening intently until I was finished.

She began, "In the beginning you were an 'unseen spectator', not yet noticed or accepted by the Spirit tribe. Yes, it was privilege for you to witness the ceremonial smoking of peyote."

"Isn't peyote the same thing as marijuana and isn't it illegal?" interrupted Hal.

Now facing Hal, Nancy continued, "Marijuana is illegal, but peyote is not, at least not on reservations. It's not even the same plant. Marijuana has leaves whereas peyote does not. It actually looks like green clusters of small gourds. Similarly, they both produce flowers that contain the mild-altering elements, but the most important difference is peyote, or the Divine Cactus, is and has always been ingested for spiritual endeavors, not recreational usage to get a buzz," now sounding a little more defensive and not pausing long, she continued. "Native Americans have perfected and used peyote in healing and ritual ceremonies since their existence. Some states tried to prohibit its use, claiming its an illegal substance, but this is a violation of the constitutional right to practice religion. The good news is, Native Americans who live on reservations, reservations being lands that fall under federal jurisdiction and not state law, are protected by the RFRA."

"What is the RFRA?" I interrupted.

She continued, "It is the Religious Freedom Restoration Act that was signed into affect by President Clinton that protects the rights of Native Americans to use peyote in religious practices. The states cannot interfere."

"Way to go Billy!" Cheered Hal. "I think it's the least the pale faces owe them since taking their land and corralling them into reservations."

"I agree!" I said, cheering on Hal's enthusiasm and sentiment.

"Let me get back on track here," Nancy pausing and shifting toward me. "Now, you were initially greeted by gray wolf, your winter Ohio totem or animal spirit guide. Representing the beginning of your journey that actually started in Ohio. By coming to Texas, you were then greeted by a western wolf. As you know, they have unique physical characteristics and from what you described, she was definitely western, which makes sense. This wolf helped you to relax, gently transitioning you to a western spirituality. You described swimming against the current of the river, though it was not difficult and you felt little or no resistance. I think this means you are experiencing a spiritual change, but find it easy. Another clue of your transition: The horse spirit is associated with both birth and death. Native Americans believe people ride in and out of this mortal world on a spiritual horse. If you look at the history of the horse, they helped people explore and find freedom, enabling them to travel. Horse brings new journeys. Finally, after being brought to a village by the horse, you were accepted by the native spirits. Amazing," she finished, nodding her head.

"That's awesome, but what about the hippo?" I asked.

"That one puzzles me, I am not sure what the significance is there, other than an animal spirit assisting you on your journey. We can consult a book when we reach our next destination."

With this last statement, I saw the road sign "Sedona 32 Miles". I was bursting with excitement. "I have heard of Sedona and always wanted to come."

"Today's your lucky day, sis," Hal said, beaming with equal excitement.

"Luck has nothing to do with it, Hal." said Nancy knowingly, "It's all in the timing."

# Chapter XII

Route 89 runs through the heart of Sedona and is lined with shops and restaurants on either side. The picturesque background of crimson cliffs and monoliths leaves one breathless. We stopped at the first specialty shop we saw, anxious to discover what Red Rock Country had to offer its' visitors. Dreamcatchers and wind chimes of all sizes were hanging in the window of the store front with a simple sign hanging on the screen door that said "Welcome".

Once inside, the familiar scent of sage could be detected and the hardwood floor told of a long history of existence. At first sight, the tiny shop was packed with native pottery and wood carvings of eagles, horses, and the famed Kokapelli, the native fertility god. Hal's attention was attracted there and this was the last I saw of him for a while. On the opposite side was a glass counter protecting jewelry made mostly of turquoise and silver with less expensive racks of bracelets and necklaces made of gemstones and a vintage cash register donning the showcase. I believe this is where I lost Nancy. I ventured on towards the back of the shop, ignoring tiny isles or paths that branched off which were marked by more wind chimes, hand-carved wooden walking sticks and garden art miniature displays. I was drawn to, at least what I thought I was, the focal point of the store. A large pyramid display of containers of local rocks and gemstones. Each compartment had their own identity card which provided the name, meaning, and use. It was obvious that they were not placed in alphabetical order, but perhaps rather what was most aesthetically pleasing to the eye. The sizes of these stones ranged from pebble to golf ball and though in different colors, all were high-gloss polished to mirror standards. I randomly chose scolecite. It "promotes inner peace and aids deep relaxation". It is a pure white-colored stone that felt just as cool as it did smooth in the palm of my hand. Rubbing absentmindedly, I rolled it into my other hand when I reached for the stone next to it. The identifying card said it was Apache tear. A polished, pure black stone that "protects against depression". It was about the same size as the scolecite but was not as flat. Next to Apache tear was red jasper. Blood red in color, it is peppered with small pronounced black flecks. It "protects against things that are bad for you". I spotted garnet next because of its texture. A black polished stone with noticeable lines or cracks like a dropped hard-boiled egg, though it is impossible to pick off the outer shell. It also looked like an old dog turd with a shine that "promotes self-confidence and fortifies courage to overcome problems". *Yup, that sounds like dog crap to me,* I thought as I chuckled and put the stone back, wiping my fingers on my jeans just in case it was the latter and not the former. Fueling my giddiness and happiness, I saw a beautiful chocolate-colored stone with rings of gold. Tiger's eye, I knew it without looking at the card. Carefully sifting through the mound of stones, I found one that fit my hand perfectly, like a proverbial glove. I know it was a stone of protection, I had seen it referenced in movies and come across it in my limited reading journeys. The card stated "promotes insight and protects from evil". It was by far the prettiest and most eye-catching stone I had seen thus far. Next to it was my least favorite stone, the unmistakable turquoise. I also knew this stone without looking at the card with its blue green color that I have always associated with Easter and embedded crevices that reminds me of a tooth cavity.

My private party soon ended when I was disrupted with a gingerly tap on the arm.

"Can I help you locate something?" she asked.

I turned my attention now to the tiny-framed, post-retirement aged clerk and probable owner.

"We have the most extensive selections of gem stones and crystal rocks in Sedona. Are you looking for anything in particular? Is this your first time visiting?"

"Nothing particular and yes, this is my first time visiting."

"Well then," speaking slowly like a preschool teacher, "some of the stones you see here also come in larger shapes of obelisks, pyramids, spheres, and eggs." She eyed the left hand that held my stones.

"No, I haven't gotten that far," I smiled and raised my open palm to proudly share with her my three stones. "I'm still browsing."

She moved closer, "Those are nice, interesting choices."

"Thank you," I continued my browsing and intentionally ignored her last statement. Something deep inside told me I did not want to know what she thought the stones meant. I wasn't done shopping and I didn't want any outside influence involved. But she continued on.

"If you are looking for love, we have malachite, rainbow jasper, amber, and pink opal," pointing at the corresponding compartments. "We also have money stones like citrine, jade, and imperial topaz."

"No thank you, I don't need any of the those," trying to be polite and move around the display, with my attention landing on the icy purple of amethyst crystals. Unlike stones, crystals are usually rectangular in shape and are not smooth but rather pointed and jagged. Their color is not solid but rather mystically cloudy. Just as I reached for a crystal, there she was again, offering unsolicited but interesting information.

"Amethyst is the crystal of spirituality and dream recall. It takes you on this transition from the magic time of dusk to a conscious shift into a different place. This crystal can show us how to let go and trust and to surrender so that you may see beyond the cycle that consumes your attention. Give it all up, so that you can receive more," and she gingerly left the way she approached.

What a strange lady.

# Chapter XIII

I went to show Nancy the stones I chose or the ones that chose me, as she would say. She had several small packets of herbs in her hand and was still searching for more.

"What did you find?" I asked with anxious curiosity as the aroma of different herbs filled my nose.

"Sage sticks for protection and purification," holding up a plastic bag with two miniature white sage sticks no bigger than highlighters, "and sweet grass to attract spirit helpers." She handed me a lengthy braiding of dried grass. It smelled sweet.

"It's amazing," she continued. "They have all kinds of dried plants, flowers, and seeds. I have never seen so many herbs in one place."

There was an entire wall dedicated to the large display of dried herbs and flowers that held numerous plastic bags stapled closed with an identification card attached. The name was in bold script on the front and the back provided its magical and medicinal properties.

"Look, they have mugwart. It enhances dreams and provides protection. By stuffing these leaves in a pillow, it is supposed to increase the frequency of the dreams as well as help to remember what those dreams were." Glancing at me and returning the packet back to its designated spot, "You don't seem to need help with that," now with a hint of pride in her smile. "I can't believe they even have willow bark," she reached to pull the packet. "Now this makes excellent tea for relieving cold and flu symptoms. It helps with fever, sore throat, and even headaches." Continuing on, "There's chickweed and licorice root used to attract love. Flax seed which lowers cholesterol and blood pressure. Coltsfoot?" Turning to read the back label, "This flower is used to promote tranquility and induce visions."

"Like peyote?" I asked with a grin spreading across my face.

"No," not seeing the humor, "It is not smoked, but rather burned as an incense." She put it back as her curiosity had been satisfied. "Anise, I want some of this," continuing on without looking at the card. "It also provides protection and purification. It is an all-purpose herb. Dried anise under a pillow is said to prevent nightmares. It can be burned as an incense for spiritual guidance or boiled and strained like tea to improve insights and deepen the inner connection. I better get two packs of this."

I smiled and was hopeful I would be a part of its usage under Nancy's tutelage. I did not want to be bothersome while she concentrated, so I left the horticulture expert and continued on exploring, perusing a smaller display of candles and oils. The "spell wax" was contained in sixteen-ounce glass cylinders with plain labels that identified different colors with names such as "Blessings of Abundance", "Blessings of Love", "Blessings of Protection", "Blessings of Purification". There were probably a dozen or so different colors and fragrances of these types of blessing candles. The oils were in much smaller glass vials with the same plain labels, but their potency more than made up for the size. They too offered assistance with harnessing desired energies. Other aromatherapy products included incense and handmade herbal soaps.

*Where's Hal?* I was overcome with a feeling that something was terribly wrong. I frantically began to look for him, surely he wouldn't forget and leave me here. The only thing worse than the feeling of abandonment was the lurking question, *Why would I feel this way?* I spotted him and my body immediately relaxed. He was in a small section devoted books and local magazines which also included a plethora of brochures on things to see and do while in Sedona.

"There you are," spying the new light tan Bushman hat that replaced his ball cap.

"Yup," with twinkles as bright in his eyes as his smile. "Do you like it?" he tipped it forward. "Look what else I found," holding up a walking stick. "Handmade, you won't find another one like it in the world, natural chestnut. See the eagle on the handle?" Now holding it at the opposite end rather than hand the entire thing over.

"Nice, the hat and the stick give you the appearance of a real explorer."

"Hey, I am a real explorer! Well, at least by heart and for this trip." He put his arm around me in that big brother protective manner. I loved it!

"Look," he continued, "They have metaphysical and spiritual services available for those looking for dream analysis, astrological readings, and energy healing. Did you see the fliers posted throughout the shop advertising for local psychics and shamanic journeys? They also have adventure tours that include hiking, kayaking on the Verde River, and western Jeep tours."

"There you two are," interrupted Nancy, who obviously needed a cart.

"We were talking about all the adventures this place has to offer," he dramatically tilted his Bushman with his stick.

"Yes, and I can see you are all prepared," she teased.

"That's right, just lead me to it. If I can't get over it or under it, I will get through it!"

"A cross between McGyver and Indiana Jones with a touch of Bud Abbott," Nancy poked.

"Probably more Abbott than anything else," he laughed along. "And it looks like you've been conquering our bank account. Here, let me help you with that," emptying most of her arms. "I'll take this up front to the register and meet you there."

Nancy held onto a book and was already turning to the glossary for assistance.

"Hippo. Here it is," finding the page. "Ancient Greek word for river horse. That makes sense, you saw the hippo in the river," thinking out loud then reading on. "The hippopotamus, sacred in Egyptian and African traditions, is the second largest mammal on earth and spends most of its day in water. This animal, very substantial in physical terms, can guide us in grounding ourselves so we can face and dissolve emotional issues. It represents the power of water. Aren't you a Pisces?" Stopping to look at me.

"Yes, what else does it say?" with renewed interest.

"The hippopotamus is associated with birth, motherhood, and the protection of young. The hippopotamus protects women of childbearing age."

"No, I am not pregnant," answering the obvious question with a look of *You gotta be kidding me!* "What else do you got?" I asked.

"While underwater, the hippopotamus is able to see, hear, and breathe. This can teach us a higher level of perception and so increases intuition for the heart and truth of situations in life."

"Now that's profound, what does it mean for me?" I asked.

"Only you can know the answer for yourself. But I am going to get you the book so you have something to reference." Turning the book to look at its cover, "It's a guide to Native American Animal Medicine and Spiritual Meanings for only $19.95." Smiling, "Besides, I can study it before you take it home."

The sudden reality of my life in Ohio felt like someone knocked the wind out of me. I forgot about that place.

Seeing this, she asked, "Are you okay?"

I stood there for what seemed a while, numb and tingling and finally answered, "I was having such a good time. I forgot we were on vacation."

Sympathetic to my disappointment, "Oh, I know. This has been a wonderful journey but it doesn't have to end here. The things we pick up, learn, and experience along the way can be used as tools when we return home. I firmly believe the cliché that 'Everything happens for a reason'. We should pay attention as the universe is always trying to tell us something and your visualization skills are terrific. Come on, let's find Hal. We've been here long enough."

Hal was trapped at the register by the strange but gentle preschool teacher, now owner.

"Oh, there they are," pulling away from her draining magnetism with a few maps in hand.

"Are you ladies ready to go?"

"Absolutely," affirmed Nancy as she placed the book on the glass counter next to the other items. "Come on Bonnie, put your stones up here too. A present from Hal and I."

Not surprisingly, the odd clerk had to comment. "You're Native American, what nation?"

"Apache," eyes smiling proudly.

"I thought so," putting the packets of lavender and sage in a brown paper bag that was quickly filling. "You seem well-versed in the use of herbs. Did you have any questions I may be able to answer?"

*I doubt it,* I thought.

"No, I believe I have all I need. Thank you," much more cordial than I would be.

She reminded me of one of those people who know a little about a lot but claims to be an expert. If you have done it, she has too. I got the nonverbal feeling that Nancy shared my sentiment that one who does not share a recipe should not try to instruct in its cooking.

As if sensing this as well, she offered, "I gave your husband a little map we have of the locations of the various vortices near us. I provide guided tours myself, but the real journey is from within. So, if this is something you want to do privately and clearly you are capable of this, then the map will assist you in locating each of the four main vortices.

"Thank you," handing her Hal's debit card.

"Just sign here," was the last she spoke to any of us.

# Chapter XIV

There was so much to experience with little time, so we knew we had to chose carefully and quickly. That did not stop us from sitting in Hal's truck looking through our bags of goodies.

"Here," from over the front seat, "I got you and Nancy matching leather pouches for your stones, crystals, and whatnots."

"That's great, thanks. Now I have a place to keep my booty."

"Oh yeah and a t-shirt. I normally don't buy t-shirts while on vacation, but this doesn't provide free advertisement for a tourist destination, just a simple airbrush picture of a soaring hawk."

"It's beautiful. Thank you. Thank you for everything. This trip has been absolutely wonderful." Holding my new shirt with pride, "Where can I change?"

"Wherever you want," laughed Hal.

I switched t-shirts within a split second of anyone realizing I was serious.

"What do you think?" pulling myself between their seats like an excited child.

"Ooh, I really like it," said Nancy. "The hawk is one of the most mystical of the birds of prey. They are the protectors, messengers, and visionaries of the air." Then looking at me as if something was missing, "Did you look in your pouch?"

"No, Hal handed me my t-shirt before I could put my stones in there," excitement growing as I pulled to loosen the leather drawstrings. Oh my goodness, it's beautiful! Words escaped me as I slowly pulled the tiger's eye necklace into view. It was a heart-shaped stone, about three by three if I had to guess, with just enough weight to know it's there without becoming burdensome or heavy.

"I love it," reaching around the seats to first hug Hal and then Nancy.

Nancy held my forearm to educate me further. "The stone as you know is tiger's eye, keep it with you. It will protect you and give you confidence to handle difficult situations. It will help you recognize self-resources that can be used for the attainment of your goals." Now holding it in her hand she admired, "Not only does it have energy properties, it is also very beautiful. It looks like a cat's eye, with its lustrous brown and yellow parallel fibers."

"What are the dark gray, shiny smaller stones that make up the chain?"

"Hematite beads. Native folklore says it was used in war paint to become invincible to one's enemies. It wouldn't lit-

erally stop a bullet, but it does show the emotional significance of what incredible faith and belief can accomplish. It
is also said to aid in the healing process."

"I will wear it always, thanks again." With tears in my
eyes, I pulled my arm from under her patting hand and slid
back into my seat so I could latch the necklace behind my
neck. I don't feel invincible? First noticing the smoothness of
the heart under my finger tips and then the exact curves that
create an unmistakable universal symbol of love.

"Let's check out this map and go visit a vortex," volunteered adventuresome Hal who was spun around in his seat,
donning the now strange-looking Bushman. "You're now
Lola. Pick one and tell me how to get there." Handing me a
folded five by eleven copier sheet. "And Nancy, you can explain what a vortex is along the way."

"It looks like the closest vortex is at what be a small
airport, which is approximately ten miles. Go west on
Route 89 and turn left on Airport Road," in my best Lola
impersonation.

"A vortex is a spiraling energy," Nancy began. "The subtle energy can be felt within a half mile of the main energy
field or vortex. The closer you get, the stronger its power.
Not only can the energy be felt, it can be seen in the trees
that grow in the areas of the vortex. The limbs are twisted in
a spiral fashion. It is quite amazing. A vortex is an excellent
place to cleanse and strengthen a person's inner being."

Before long, Hal's truck was traveling up a winding road
that led to the airport vortex.

"There are two entrances to the trails that will lead us through the vortex. Park at the first one you see." My excitement was growing.

Standing in front of a wooden sign proclaiming "Airport Vortex", I motioned them to follow up the trail to the left. "This looks like a path less taken. It looks like most people follow the path to the right, but this," now walking single file picking our way through the small shrubs to locate the unused trail, "will lead us some place special."

The path continued winding its way to the east edge of a crimson cliff where there was suddenly no vegetation, just rock. We paused for a moment.

"Are you sure this is the way Lola?" joked Hal, stretching his neck to look down over the edge. "Nancy is afraid of heights," he continued nervously, "and she doesn't have a walking stick like me."

"Don't worry about me," Nancy replied quickly with her hand holding the back of Hal's belt. "I don't look over the edge." Pointing, "see there are small bunches of wild sage scattered on the mountainside. What good luck, that will provide to be useful later after its been dried. Hal, don't let me forget to pick some before we leave."

"Don't worry, I even remembered to grab a Ziplock bag for you," magically pulling it from his front shirt pocket. "I figured she would find something interesting," following me further along the edge.

"You make a great assistant Hal," I heard Nancy praise loudly from the rear.

We came upon the opening edge of an enormous rock. In unison, "Wow" came from next to me instead of behind me.

"I can't believe how much space there is. The view from the road is deceiving. I didn't know the other side was a canyon of red rock that opened a view of the entire state of Arizona," Hal became giddier the more he spoke. "I don't know if it's the altitude, you know, thin air," now looking ridiculously funny with his crooked Bushman, "but I feel a bit strange. Light. Light-headed. No, light-hearted." Turning to face the mountainside as if he were its conductor in a symphony, arms raised with the walking stick in one hand, "I feel great!"

"Could it be the vortex?" I was thinking out loud.

"No doubt there is an energy present, look at the juniper tree," Nancy said, stepping past Hal to get a closer look at the miniature tree.

The tree reminded me of an over-sized bonsai tree with its long branches and small cluster of leaves.

"Look at the branches," she continued. "See how they are twisted in a spiral fashion? They are twisted from the energy, the spiraling energy that comes from Mother Earth which creates a vortex. On the spiritual side, the energy of the vortices interact with whom or what a person is in their inner self. It resonates with and strengthens the Inner Being of each person. This resonance occurs because the vortex energy is very similar to the subtle energy operating in the energy centers inside each person. A place where the subtle force between Mother Nature and man converge."

"We can't waste this spectacular scenery and the path has been clear so far. I think we need a good cleansing. How about it Nancy?" encouraged Hal.

"I can't think of a better place to try out this new smudge stick," pulling the miniature cigar from her new pouch. "Bonnie, you go first."

I assumed the position facing outward over the cliff. Feet shoulder-width apart, shoulders relaxed, eyes closed, and mind open. I could hear them behind me trying to keep the lighter lit long enough to ignite the sage.

"Stand there to block the wind," Hal instructed Nancy who quickly took over once the sage began to smolder.

"Remember, deep inhale through the nose and slow exhale through the mouth. As you take that deep breath, visualize the air as white, clean, and fresh. As you exhale, visualize your breath as dark or dirty. The air is cleansing your body and spirit and with each breath you feel lighter."

I was in a groove, easily visualizing as Nancy spoke when all of the sudden, I felt a stinging pain on my right shoulder. It was the kind of unexpected pain that causes instinctive reflexes to grab at the area. Hot!

"Oh no," Nancy was now tugging at my shirt. "I am so sorry. An ember must have blown off the stick and I did not realize it. Are you okay? Did you get burned?"

"I'm fine. It's not your fault, really," trying to reassure her. "It gives my shirt character and me a good story to share. You two get yourselves cleansed and I'm going to sit down over there and enjoy the view."

The spot I chose was perfect. A huge flat rock that hung over the cliff's edge. As close to a bird's eye view as one can get without leaving the ground. All of the famous monoliths could be seen as backdrop to the picturesque Sedona. The ground beneath my Indian-style seat was literally rock hard, but I could feel its warmth through my jeans. The sun was bright with not a cloud in the sky, but the breeze kept it cool. I closed my eyes and let my senses soak up the atmosphere, visualizing white spiraling light surrounding me. We sat for a long while on the cliff's edge, sitting quietly as we meditated. I could have slept there, maybe I did.

# CHAPTER XV

From Sedona, we were on the move again up Route 64, making our way north to the Grand Canyon. "Since it's right here," as Hal would say. We wanted to get an early start as time was rapidly slipping away and we had to return to our 'real' worlds soon, so we were limited to one day at the national park. The toll booths were manned by uniformed rangers that at first glance immediately reminded me of the famed Smokey Bear who preached forest fire prevention. This and an entrance guarded by enormous trees one would find in an ancient forest was deceiving as to what lied beneath. We entered the park at the South Rim, stopping at the first point of interest called Mather Point.

"Wow," was once again all that could be heard or spoken when the canyon finally came into view. Grand is an understated adjective when describing this great chasm carved through the rocks of the Colorado Plateau. Though I have seen pictures but nothing compared to actually being here.

As if in a trance, we all got out of the truck and were invisibly being pulled up to the rocky rim of this humbling vast visual expression of time. We stood in silence for some time, scanning this seemingly infinite world, the senses drinking in the sun and gentle breeze. It reminded me of airport vortex in Sedona, but on a much larger scale. I heard my name from behind and when I turned to look, Hal and Nancy were already standing at their opened doors.

"Sorry, I was caught up in the beauty," quickly walking towards Hal's truck.

"I know what you mean, it's kind of a shock to the system when you first see it. I felt overwhelmed," commiserated Nancy, who was slowly shaking her head in disbelief.

Handing me a canyon guide, Hal said, "I even walked over to the visitor's center. I bet you didn't notice I was gone."

"No, I didn't," feeling as though I had lost conscious time.

"See, I could have fell off the side o the canyon and you wouldn't have known it," laughed Hal.

Nancy, not so amused, countered, "With the stone barriers and common sense, there is no reason you should fall off and it's not funny to joke about!"

"Okay, on to the next stop," Hal changed the subject. "Bonnie what does the canyon guide say?"

Me not finished with our banter. "I can't hear it," holding the guide to my ear. "It's not talking."

"Very funny," looking at me in the rearview mirror. "Maybe I should turn left," motioning towards the side window which framed only a portion of the vastness of the canyon.

"That's a long way down. I would not suggest that route." With my attention to the map on the back of the guide I announced, "Next stop, Grandview Point. There is a North Rim and a South Rim, which is what we are on. Services include camping, lodging, restaurants, and a free shuttle bus system." I continued reading aloud, "It says the average distance across the canyon is ten miles, as 'the condor flies'. However, the drive from the North Rim to the South Rim is five and a half hours, or 215 miles."

"Ten miles," Hal said in disbelief. "It looks like it's a lot further than that. Are you sure you're reading that correctly?"

"That's what it says," pointing to the factoid as if he was sitting next to me rather than in the front seat driving. "As the condor flies? I wonder what that means, Nancy?" I questioned.

"I'm not sure where the phrase originated. But in my native language, a condor is a type of vulture, the king of buzzards so to speak. If I'm not mistaken, the world's largest flying bird. They are usually associated with ugliness and death but they are actually symbols of purification, new vision, death, and rebirth. Yes, they may pick the carcass of a dead animal clean, but this means of survival prevents the spread of disease and keeps the circle of life in balance. Native American's used their feathers in rituals for grounding after ceremonies, helping to return to this world. On a practical level, you are right Hal. It would be a lot further than ten miles across the canyon but..."

Hal finished, "if the Condor is the largest flying bird, ten miles for him would realistically be what, a bazillion miles for us?" Sounding proud of himself.

"Bazillion, how far is that?" I asked. "And of more interest, what does death and rebirth have to do with the Grand Canyon?"

My last question was left hanging in the air as we entered the parking area at Grandview Point. It was as awe-inspiring as Mather's Point. The immense enormity of the canyon was making me feel light-headed and it felt as if my depth perception was way off, so I did not venture too close to the edge. My brother Hal, on the other hand, approached with the excitement and lack of concern as a little boy when he jumped up on the rock guard rail.

"Take my picture, take my picture Nancy!" he squealed with delight.

"Hal, that is not funny! Get down from there!" turning her back so as not to see him.

The puzzled look on his face showed how invulnerable he really felt he was. "Oh Nancy," squatting to his feet to climb down, "Don't be afraid, I was just having fun."

"I told you at the last stop to stay away from the edge," chastising Hal with tears welling in her eyes.

"I'm sorry bunny," he whispered in her ear as he tried putting his arm around her. "It won't happen again," he promised.

Pulling away from his attempted embrace, we followed her back to the truck. Her rejection at his apology clearly annoyed him.

"Maybe we should think about heading home," Hal said as he climbed behind the driver's wheel. We both ignored him. He started he truck and put it in gear.

Focusing on her surroundings or being a good co-pilot, Nancy warned, "You should wait for that guy to finish parking."

"I see him. I hope he sees me," growling at her. Then a small thump. "Hey, wait… He just hit me."

"I guess he didn't see you," I light-heartedly remarked.

He ignored my attempt at humor. "I can't believe this!" Hal said as he pushed the door open to dismount and survey the unlikely damage.

Hal met an elderly white-haired man at the back of his camper and the front of his truck. Like watching a silent movie at a drive-in, the obvious charm of the seasoned tourist was tempering my brother, so I carefully asked Nancy, "Why did you get so upset with Hal for getting up on the rock? Are you afraid of heights?"

Taking a moment, "No, I'm not afraid of heights." And as if keeping a secret, she further offered, "He just scares me sometimes. I got angry because I asked him the very first area we stopped at to please stay away from the edge. He was just trying to prove a point and that's what angered me the most."

I wondered, she was not afraid of heights, this I believed. She had dreams of flight and was excited, not fearful, when she talked about them. Hal was clearly not in any eminent danger, so where was this fear coming from?

Hal was returning to get back in the truck with no hard feelings and I did not want to be obvious of our topic of conversation so I slid back into my seat to once again thumb through the free guide provided by park services.

"Just scratched the license plate is all," he put the truck in gear again. "It was no big deal. He was a really nice guy. He and his family are from Florida." Getting no indication that Nancy was over his rock-hopping stunt, he stopped sharing information on his new-found friend and quietly pulled back onto Route 64.

It was not long before I broke the silence and offered, "There are several more areas where we can stop for the same breathtaking views. But since our time is limited, how about we just skip them and stop at the last area called Desert View. Here they have a watchtower to tour, a trading post, and, most importantly, a restroom."

"That sounds good to me," Hal sounded more upbeat.

"Me too," agreed Nancy.

Adding more energy to the melting tension, I ended with "Then that will take us to the east exit of the park and on our way home."

"Yeeha!" chimed Hal as he patted Nancy's thigh.

She replied with a large smile and gave his hand a reassuring pat. Looking back at me and wanting to be either more involved or more informed asked, "Let me look at that guide Hal picked up."

I handed it over the front seat and relaxed back into my leather seat, watching the scenery from my window as the tepid breeze blew the hair from my searching eyes. I was startled by Nancy playfully smacking Hal with the guide.

"See, I told you Hal, do not get too close to the edge." Opening the guide, she pointed to a column titled "Use Caution Near the Edge". She continues reading aloud, "Rock-hopping outside the guard rails leads to tragic fall. A man dies after he falls while trying to get to a rock outcrop for a photograph. What was to be a memorable vacation becomes a nightmare for the family and friends of the victim. He was probably joking too." Her anger had changed to teasing. But when you love someone, there was and always will be concern.

Of course, I had to add, "Yeah, and you know what happens when you don't listen to the wise one?"

Hal's confused eyes in the mirror, waiting for an answer.

"Someone backs into your nice truck," I playfully snickered. He laughed and shook his head while I continued. "See, Nancy warned you to stay away from the edge and rather than take it seriously, you pulled that stunt. That was karma getting you back when the guy backed into you. This time it was a scratched license plate, next time who knows?"

Laughing, Nancy leaned into him pointing, "That's right buster, you had better listen to me."

# CHAPTER XVI

I t was nice to see them enjoying each other again and right before our last stop, for which we had just arrived. Desert View, though with the ample parking in front, it could have been mistaken for Asphalt View. The huge parking lot was scattered with clusters of cars for last stop viewing and shopping. We found a spot in the shade far from any other vehicles that I was sure to point out to Hal. We had just gotten out of the truck when we were greeted by a large rather verbose crow.

"Where did he come from?" Hal was quicker than I.

"How do you know it's a he?" I retorted.

"The size, it's too big for a female. Nancy grab me those cheese snacks. I bet he's hungry," egging me on.

The bird must have understood the last statement because now it was hopping towards us, head down, wings spread and cawing.

"A smart bird, she must be a female," I jabbed back.

"You're right, she must be a female," he finally conceded.

"She only quits squawking when she has food in her mouth."

This was one big bird, like none I have been so close to before. Her striking black feathers with hints of deep blue and purple. Her beak as black and shiny as her talons. Black, watchful eyes as she cocked her head from side to side as if listening to hear a secret.

"Ha, ha, you are a comedian, my brother," I laughed. "You are right in that she is female, she is too pretty to be anything but," now talking to the bird.

She was not skittish by any means. She was actually down right bossy, cawing if Hal did not throw her another cheese puff before she was done swallowing what she already had.

"Uh oh, now she has competition," Nancy pointed out as a second but larger bird approached.

"Now, I bet that's the male," Hal said as he threw a cheese puff past the waiting female.

"You're probably right," I teased. "The male waited for the female to coax a snack and comes in at the end to claim a prize. He must be her brother," ending our sibling banter.

Hal quickly emptied the last crumbs from the bag and proclaimed, "All gone. Now let's go before we draw more and there is a showdown."

"Yeah, crows seem more aggressive than their cousin the magpie. We met them at the Petrified Forest, remember?" I asked.

"That's right, good memory," said Nancy. "Those were magpies, but these two are not crows, they are ravens.

"What's the difference?" I asked.

"In appearance, the size. When Hal commented on she being a he, I thought he was right. But when I saw the second bird, I knew they must be ravens. Crows are not that big, even if they are over-fed by tourists. They are both scavenger species, able to adapt and survive the environment. They are both pitch black, which is the obvious color of night. Metaphorically, black night gives birth to a new day. They are playful and not intimidated easily, which makes them less vulnerable to prey. It is said that 'nestled in midnight wings of the raven are messages beyond space and time and come only to those within the tribe who are worthy of knowledge.' It is the Native American bearer of magic and deliverer of messages. It is also a keeper of secrets and can help in determining answers to our own hidden thoughts. Hidden as in areas of our lives that we are unwilling to face or secrets we keep that harm us."

The discussion of the ravens kept our attention preoccupied until we reached the end of the concrete sidewalk, which was the canyon or Desert View. No matter what angle, the initial view is breathtaking and leaves most speechless for quite some time. Standing on the unguarded edge of the canyon and looking out at its beauty, I wondered how many people jumped to their death. I wondered how may thought that if they did jump, they could fly. I wondered, can I fly?

# Chapter XVII

Far off in the distance I hear faint crying. My eyelids too heavy to open, I lay listening to the sounds of my breath. The crying becomes louder, a faint female voice.

"Just let me keep my music. Please."

"We don't allow electronic devices."

"Please! It doesn't use internet." Sobbing, "The music helps me. I need it."

"This one goes to Room 722," an annoyed woman's voice.

"No, please! Why won't you listen? I can't be alone with my thoughts. I need my music. I won't bother anyone, I promise. Please!"

The voices faded and it was quiet again.

# Chapter XVIII

I t seemed only minutes before I was awakened again to the sound of that barking little dog. *Not again,* I thought as I reached for the reading light chain. I felt oddly lethargic, which is probably why I didn't notice that the chain was much longer, there was no headboard, and the floor I was now standing on was not carpeted. I fumbled toward the light behind the door and slowly stepped around, still holding the handle for balance. Suddenly I was at the end of a hallway with numbered rooms along both sides. *My God was I in an accident?* I thought as I looked down my body. No obvious wounds but I was barefoot and wearing light blue hospital scrubs. I don't remember what happened. I had no recent memory, my heart was pounding, and my head spinning, yet my movement was very slow. It felt as if I was walking in quick sand and every step was in slow-motion. Halfway down the hall I found a nurse's station.

Not able to get the words out of my mouth fast enough, "Where am I, what happened?" I asked the stout nurse with long black braided hair who was sitting behind the gray counter protected by Plexiglas.

Glancing up, she coldly and matter-of-factly responded with pudgy jowls, "Flower Hospital," and returned her focus to the chart sitting in front of her.

"What happened? Why am I here?" trying not to sound desperate.

Without looking up, "Your doctor will be in to see you later." Then a pause and another glance to let me know this was it, she ended with, "You can discuss your status with her then."

Even in all my confusion, this encounter seemed familiar to me as did the brown-skinned nurse. Nonetheless, I did not care for her flippant attitude but I did not have the physical or emotional strength to question her further about just exactly what was my "status". Besides, I don't think she would have given me anymore information. I must be on some heavy duty pain killers.

I heard the barking of the dog again and slowly followed the noise further down the hall. I was no longer annoyed by it, but was hopeful it would awaken me from what seems to be a strange dream. I came to a small room surrounded by glass walls that was occupied by a thin elderly patient smoking a cigarette. In between long shaky drags, he would mimic the sound of a small barking dog. I stood staring at this man with surprise. I was expecting instead to be looking at a dog. He had short gray hair and a rather large pronounced curved nose. He too had a familiarity that was just out of reach of my mental grasp.

Finally, this is too weird and I'm exhausted. I need to get back to my bed to wake from this dream or to get some answers. In a fog, I made my way back past the nurse's station to the end of the hall. I was unsure if this room with the twin size bed was mine, but felt instinctively that it was so I laid down. Besides, if this was a dream it really didn't matter and the solace of that notion allowed me to quickly fall asleep.

# CHAPTER XIX

The upbeat five knock Morse code and "Yoooohoooo, hellooooo", woke me from my sleep.

An impish face peeking around the closed door, "Breakfast is here, are you going to eat today?" and then sliding into full view but careful not to cross a self-evident imaginary line.

"Um, yes," realizing I was famished as I stretched.

As if finding a new friend, "I'm Autumn and you can sit by me or us. I figured you must be hungry," as if reading my stomach's mind. Her vibrant energy a bit annoying to me as she bounced out of the room.

Out in the common area sat a dozen or so other people dressed in the same light blue scrubs I was wearing.

Still getting my bearings, Autumn waived and called, "Over here, I saved you a seat. Got your breakfast tray too." I went to the round table where she was sitting as she pushed a chair out with her foot. Rubbing my eyes and trying to grasp my surroundings, she interrupted. "This is Crystal, that's Jennifer and that's Fred."

Still confused, I said "Hi," and took my seat without making eye contact.

"Hi," said Fred.

Autumn continued, "The food here's pretty good."

"Pretty good," said Fred.

Ignoring Fred, Autumn added, "You have to fill out a menu each morning."

"Each morning," said Fred.

Again, Autumn continued, "But if nothing looks good, then you can write what you want instead. See," showing me the menu that was on her tray. "Oh yeah, and if there is anything you don't want, keep it. We put it in the refrigerator for a snack later."

"In the refrigerator for a snack later," said Fred.

Leaning closer, Autumn informed me, "Ignore Fred, he likes to repeat everything he hears. Which reminds me, if you smoke, we have a room for that too.

Rather than mimic Autumn, Fred deviated and said, "The only one in the State," followed by a dog bark.

I did not feel much like being sociable and simply nodded my head.

"Okay Fred, that's enough. Finish your breakfast!" chastised Crystal.

For the first time that I took the time to look at her, I noticed Crystal and her dark, damp aura that was anything like her name. Her skin was pasty white and she had dark circles around her eyes. She appeared to have the unseen weight of the world on her shoulders.

Under the cover of my Styrofoam plate laid watery scrambled eggs and limp wheat toast. There was a carton of 2% milk and a cup of hot tea.

"You have a low-calorie, no-taste meal," Jennifer observed. "They give that to everyone just coming in and to people who don't fill out a menu. I came in late last night so I have the same." Pulling back her long blonde hair, she revealed tired blue eyes. "I can't believe we are not even allowed hair ties. Belts and hoodie strings I can understand, but hair ties and even shoe laces? Now that's crazy!"

With annoyance, Crystal added, "Which is why they took your Walkman when you got here last night."

"No, they said they took it because it was an electronic device, which is why I brought it instead of my iPhone. They didn't care and would not listen to me."

"Would not listen to me," interrupted Fred, followed with a bark.

"Fred!" Crystal snapped and then went on to explain further, "I get really tired of hearing him, especially when he wakes everyone up with that God damn barking."

"Maybe you need stronger meds so you can sleep," offered Autumn with sincere humor.

This last statement struck a nerve with me as a tingling sensation traveled down my neck. *What am I doing here?* Feeling alone and confused, I left the area and breakfast without saying another word. One thing for certain, I wasn't going to say much until I figured out what was going on.

# Chapter XX

Afternoon brought out a different crowd, as I would soon learn. I met Randy, a gay man who was apparently depressed or perhaps even gender confused, though he does sport a rather handsome beard. He reminded me of the flight attendant in his passive aggressive, stereotypical disposition or "genteel charm" as he would call it. He was short in stature, but commanded a decent audience when he was sociable. A bit of a pill freak, always asking for drugs to dull the pain in his left leg that was currently encased in a splint.

"Do you want to play?" was the first he spoke to me.

"No thanks, I'm not much for playing cards."

"There's not much else to do up here on the weekends. There is only one mandatory group at 2:00 today. You're welcome to have a seat and watch."

"Thanks," as I pulled out a chair to sit.

Soon Autumn was bouncing down the hall from where I assume was her room because she had a serious case of bed-head. She must have been sleeping. Seeing the light click on, her eyes lit up and she made her way to Randy who was sitting with his leg propped up on another chair.

"Hello sleepy," as she leaned down to kiss him on the cheek and rub his shoulder. "Who's winning, can I play next?" From zero to sixty in a matter of seconds, she hopped in one of the empty chairs centered around the four-player euchre game. "I like your necklace. Tiger's eye, isn't it?" she called from across the table.

"Yes, it is," touching it quickly. I forgot about it and was thankful it was real. I could feel my heart race.

"I don't know much about that stuff, but I do know tiger's eye is for protection, right? You and Teacher will get along just dandy," rocking in her seat.

I was scared to ask, "Who's Teacher?"

"Oh girl, you haven't met her yet?" Randy touched my arm with the fingertips of his arched wrist. "Sweet, but boy be careful, if this one gets you cornered she will talk your ear off." Now flamboyantly rolling his eyes, "You'll recognize her when you see her." Checking his watch, "She should be here shortly."

"Whose deal? I'm in now," called Autumn, who looked tiny in her over-sized scrubs.

"Hey, I wanna play too," called Jennifer, who appeared from behind a gathered group.

"Dawn, you were supposed to get me when you were ready to play," she said rejected, hands on hips.

"I'm sorry sweetie. Here, slide in right there," Autumn said, making amends. "Excuse me," dramatically grunting, "Can I get this chair by you? Thanks. Here Jennifer, sit."

I felt the need to stretch my legs, but more than that, to get away from the group that seemed to be growing larger and more familiar. The social room was the main gathering area and where meals were eaten. I found a chair by a window at the opposite end of the hall. It looked warm outside. I don't know how long I sat there. Quite some time, I imagine. Then I was interrupted with a gingerly tap on the arm.

"Hello, my name is Gloria. I like your necklace. I like the shape of it," speaking slow and deliberate. "I have a tiger's eye egg that I picked up in New Mexico. Where did you find yours?" Gently initiating conversation. Unlike everyone else I met, she was wearing no-brand name jeans, a pink summer top, and white canvas slip-on shoes. Her hair was short and well groomed. She wore "cheater" reading glasses on the end of her nose.

"It is a gift from my brother."

"Hmm, like he's protecting you with his love. I like it! You know, different stones have different uses and often overlap. They find us at certain times in our lives, whether we realize it or not. Some for protection and some for healing. I call this my ying-yang charm." She pulled a necklace from beneath her shirt. "It's made of scolecite, the white stone, which promotes inner peace and aids in deep relaxation and Apache tear, the black stone that protects against depression. It is said that Apache tear came to be when the Apache women mourned the loss of their men in battle and their tears froze to the ground, thereby creating the black glass. According to native lore, anyone who carries this stone does not feel the need to mourn because the Apache women mourned enough loss."

"It's pretty. Where did you find it?" I asked.

"I ordered it online. Had it special made for myself," looking down at it with pride. "Then there's crystals," she tucked her charm safely back under her shirt. "They are much more magical than stones. My favorite is rose quartz, which of course is pink, a cloudy light pink. It is very powerful," smiling to herself. "And one should be careful not to interfere with the path of another," now serious, "No matter how tempting." Clearly there was a story here, but she did not seem willing to share. Instead she continued, "Now amethyst, it is the crystal of spirituality and dream recall. It can show how to let go and trust, to surrender so that you may see beyond the cycle that consumes your attention."

Ignoring the familiarity of this statement, I instead asked, "How is it that you know so much about stones and crystals?"

"Self-taught through books and travel. It is my dream to semi-retire and open a little metaphysical shop somewhere in Arizona."

"I could see you doing that," I agreed.

"Really?" she was openly pleased.

"Yes."

I still wasn't sure what was going on, but I was still digesting my surroundings and my memory was becoming clearer, albeit still strange.

# CHAPTER XXI

People began filing into the small room, taking seats in chairs set up in a circle.

"Hello, my name is Reuben. I am a nurse and I will be facilitating today's group."

Reuben was tall, even sitting in a chair he towered over most of the people. A gentle giant, his eyes were kind and he had a comforting tone of voice. His thinning hair and white mustache were the only signs of aging.

"For those who are new, you are not required to participate. However, I do ask that you be respectful of the others, listening without judging and raising your hand to speak. We will go around the room and introduce ourselves, sharing as much information as you feel comfortable."

"I'll start," he squirmed in his chair and raised his hand as an after-thought. "Hi, my name is Steve and as you can tell from my street clothes, I am hoping to be released today."

He was the only person who was wearing jeans, a t-shirt, and shoes. I chuckled when I noticed his Nike high-tops did not have shoe laces to contain the wild tongues. *You're not released yet,* I thought. He was high-strung but I guess this could easily be attributed to his excitement at being discharged. His short brown hair was disheveled and his brown eyes wide.

"Congratulations Steve," said Reuben. "I see you're an Eagles' fan," nodding to his vintage 1977 Hotel California concert tour t-shirt.

"He's an Eagles' fan," interrupted Fred.

"You bet I am!" he gave a pinky and thumb sign with both hands. "Rock on dude! You look like a rock and roller yourself Reuben. Why I would even guess you play guitar?"

"I am and I do," a smile revealing a missing left incisor. "I also know you are not old enough to have attended the concert. Where did you get the shirt?"

"I got it at the head shop," he said with a devilish grin. "They have all kinds of reprinted old rock band t-shirts. And cheap too."

"What's a head shop?" asked Autumn, without raising her hand.

"It's where they sell weed paraphernalia and hippy crap," chimed in Randy who was dramatically rolling his eyes.

"Oh, like bongs and pipes to smoke pot," confirmed Autumn.

"Like bongs and pipes," mimicked Fred, followed by a bark.

"Okay, we are getting a little off-track now," said Reuben, who was immediately ignored by Steve. "Hey, the legalization of medical and personal marijuana usage barely failed. It will be legal one day. It has medicinal purposes. I know it makes me less nervous to be around people and I can focus much better."

"It makes me paranoid," chided Randy.

Ignoring Randy too, Steve continued, "Studies show there are no long-term effects from smoking pot either. Oh, and the Native American's use it for their religion." Giving an affirmative nod and sliding back into his seat, he ended his endorsement.

"Okay people, this is not a political forum. We need to change topics and remember to raise our hands before taking a turn to speak," said Reuben, trying to gain control of the conversation.

"Not a political forum," said Fred, who was sitting to the left of Steve.

"Let's go clockwise. Fred, is there anything you would like to add?" asked Reuben gently.

There was no verbal response, but physically his thin frame was rocking back and forth in his chair and his watchful eyes remained searching without making eye contact with anyone.

"Okay, next," nodding to a plump black woman who with the exception of her face and short, spiked blonde hair poking out the top was entirely wrapped in a blanket.

"My name is Tameka Jones and I just got here, so I'm gonna pass," yawning as she pulled the blanket around her cheeks, shutting out everyone in the room.

"Tameka Jones," said Fred.

Without cue, "Hi, my name is Al and I have obsessive compulsive disorder." He too was rather portly and had rosy cheeks but most noticeable was the horrible toupee he was sporting. Brown and course with a part right down the middle. *So unattractive,* I thought and kind of familiar.

"I have been here three days to get my medication adjusted." Suddenly quiet, studying his simultaneous hands as each finger touched his thumb. Distracted by counting, he said no more. I was surprised Fred did not respond to Al, like a quiet alliance.

Autumn was up next, leaping from her seat. "As you all know, my name is Autumn and I am bipolar type I. More manic than depressive if you couldn't tell," smiling from ear to ear.

"More manic than depressive," chimed in Fred, followed by a bark.

"Tell it girl," encouraged Randy as he slid up his seat to attention. His body language was obvious for those he liked and disliked.

Still standing, "I live with my mom right now, she helps me with my money. I'm here because my medication stopped working."

"It stopped working," added Fred.

"What do you mean it stopped working?" asked Rueben. "What were you taking?"

Now sitting on one leg, "Well, I was on lithium and then Depakote," standing once again looking off in the distance. "Now I'm taking Seroquel." Sitting down and jumping back up, "And Klonopin for immediate relief when I'm feeling manic."

*Like now!* I thought.

"Oh, Klonopin is a nice drug," Randy was now fully alert and feeding off Autumn's high energy. Now standing, "I have anxiety and depression issues, which is why I have no time for other people's drama."

*No, you're just a prick,* I thought. *I haven't seen anyone here take any medications.*

"I have used Klonopin for panic attacks but my doctor stopped prescribing them for me. Said something about being addictive. Hey, I say if there is a pill out there to make you feel better, then TAKE it!" He said, now looking at Jennifer.

"Hey," Jennifer stood to face him nose-to-nose, "I get tired of taking the medicine. It makes me tired and it doesn't always work. Unlike you and many others here, I don't have a family. I live in a shitty group home." She tearfully took a seat, "and I have voices that keep a running dialogue in my mind," she head was now in both hands. "Schizoaffective is my diagnosis."

For the first time, Randy finally seemed genuinely affected by her pain and even tried to comfort her. "Everyone goes off their meds, it's nothing to be ashamed of. Hell, I go off my meds all the time."

Fred was also affected by her desperation, so much so he got off his perch and left the group.

Watching this unfold, I did not notice the tears in her eyes until she spoke next, "I'm Crystal. I don't hear voices but I do get depressed." Her body language and monotone speech showed she was an empty and sad creature. "I don't have insurance or money, so I haven't had medication for..." Tears rolled down her cheeks. "Some days it is really hard to get out of bed and some days it's hard to find a reason to live. Then I came here." She wiped away her tears.

I was last in this circle of noncompliance and simply said, "I have nothing to add."

# Chapter XXII

Alone in my room, I did not hear her enter.

"Good afternoon Bonnie, how are you doing today?"

The sense of familiarity in her voice overwhelmed me to the point of feeling dizzy. Turning to meet her gaze, I remembered she looked similar to my sister-in-law with her brown skin, black hair, high cheekbones, and deep eyes.

"Very confused. I'm not quite sure why I'm here, other than maybe a little loss of memory."

"I see you refused your medicine yesterday," flipping through my chart as she sat in a chair at the end of the bed. "Why did you do that?"

"As I said," becoming a bit agitated, "I am very confused as to why I am here. I don't think it wise to take medications that one, make me extremely drowsy and two, I have no idea what these medications are being used for. And I'm not the only one here not taking the meds."

"Do you remember being admitted?"

"No, I don't. I couldn't tell you how long I have been

here, which is another reason I didn't want the medication."

"What is the last you do remember?" She was emotionless.

"As I mentioned, my memory was a bit hazy but since I stopped taking the medicine, things have become clearer. Being here has triggered what I do remember last and that was a vacation with my brother Hal and his wife Nancy."

"What do you mean being here has triggered your memory?" Now with more interest.

"Actually, it's very strange. The people I have met here and conversations I have had are similar to the experiences on the trip."

"For example?" She gently prodded.

"The barking dog," reflecting back on my first day in the hospital.

"Did you say 'barking dog'?" with surprise in her voice.

"Yes, the first day here and the first morning at my brother's house I was woken up by a barking dog. Well, it was a barking dog in Texas and here it was Fred. Fred mimics people and physically even resembles my brother's African Grey Smokey. I also noticed that other patients resemble his canaries, one with spiked yellow feathers, one with male pattern baldness, and one with that God-awful toupee!"

"Birds with male pattern baldness and toupees?" She was now looking at me over the chart. "Anyone else you noticed?" with slight sarcasm in her voice.

"Well, yes. Autumn. She reminds me of the gal in Texas who tended to my brother's birds and other pets when we went on our trip. She was off the charts like Dawn, very animated and high strung. They also have similar physical characteristics."

"Do they both work at the post office?" she asked.

"I don't have a clue," very puzzled. I never told her where Dawn worked. I continued, "Steve reminded me of our stop in Winslow, Arizona. He was wearing a vintage Eagles t-shirt and my brother was learning to play the guitar. So that was a nice unexpected detour for both of us"."

"So, you play guitar too?"

"I haven't in years. Why do you ask?" I asked, confused.

"I assumed because you just said it was an unexpected detour for you both that it meant you both play guitar."

*When was the last time I picked up my guitar?* I wondered, but not for long.

"Then there's Randy," like I was getting ready to spill a secret. "He reminds me of the unsympathetic steward from the plane that flew me to Texas. They were both indifferent to the unfortunate congenital suffering of others. First, the little girl on the plane and then Jennifer here in group. I don't care for him. He warned me about Gloria, who I just love!"

"Who is Gloria?" she asked.

"A lady here they call 'Teacher'. She was a shop owner in Sedona."

"A lady here owned a shop in Sedona, Arizona?" she sounded confused.

"No, she just reminded me of a lady that owned a shop in Sedona where we visited. They both have the same matronly physical appearance. They even sound the same."

"What do you mean?"

"They both have a large knowledge base of gemstones and crystals and a certain way of talking about them, providing their names and powers. It's hard for me to describe. She even chose the same stones I did," I said, remembering her ying and yang necklace and now feeling for my own amulet that was absent. It must be with my clothes and other personal items.

"What about your brother and sister-in-law, anyone remind you of them?"

"My brother," speaking as if thinking out loud. "The nurse Reuben has his physique and gentle demeanor. He tried his best to get me to take medicine last night, telling me Haldol was my friend. When is Haldol prescribed?"

"Anyone remind you of your sister-in-law?" she said, ignoring my last question.

"Yes, you. There is a familiarity that I can't put my finger on."

"Me?" Surprised.

"Yes, your physical appearance is similar and as a physician, you should be knowledgeable and insightful like Nancy."

"I see," pausing to look into my eyes as if she was trying to figure something out. "You know, I prescribe medications for a good reason and I am concerned that you are refusing to take your medications."

"Look," cutting her off, "I think I am better without the medication and have proven that by being able to connect the dots for you."

I was relieved, even proud, that I solved the puzzle that was my current life and felt extremely agitated that she invalidated my findings by skipping right to the drugs. I figured out what was going on and even laid the road map for the doctor.

"I appreciate that, but the dots you are connecting are based on your hallucinations and not real-life experiences. You asked me what Haldol was prescribed for and it is to lessen hallucinations. I am familiar to you because I have treated you for the past five years and Haldol, when taken, works best for you."

"I don't understand. Are you saying that it is because I stopped taking the meds that I was able to remember what happened prior to me being admitted?"

"What I am saying," she said slowly, "Is the trip never happened."

"That's bullshit," I said with total disbelief.

"Even by your own admission, the patients her account for the people you met on your trip and the people here shows you the negative impacts of not taking prescribed medications."

Closing my eyes, there was an overwhelming smell of sage and I began questioning my own reality.

"All of my senses were engaged in a hallucination? What I saw, what I felt and what I smelled? I don't believe you." I took long pause to collect my thoughts. "But if what you are saying is true, then I went on the trip before I came here and before I met the other patients. That would not be possible." Now with anger, "My reality, just like every other human being, is what I believe it to be and I refuse to believe your interpretation!"

"Your trip was an analogy," she said, studying me.

"An analogy, I don't understand."

"Life and death," she was still studying me, "All the places you visited with your brother."

"My brother?" I was still not following her.

"Yes, when he traded his ball cap for a Bushman hat," as if she was dropping another hint. Still trying to comprehend what she was trying to say, she hit me with this statement. "Your brother's name was James and he was killed in an automobile accident five years ago. We go through this every year Bonnie, when you stop taking your medication."

The words hung in the air, echoing in my ears. Then it went dark again.